A COCKTAIL TO DIE FOR

A RIGHT ROYAL COZY INVESTIGATION
MYSTERY

HELEN GOLDEN

DREW BRADLEY PRESS

ALSO BY HELEN GOLDEN

ISBN (P) 978-1-915747-16-7

Edited by Marina Grout at Writing Evolution

Published by Drew Bradley Press

Cover design by Helen Drew-Bradley

First edition November 2023

To Pete,
I am proud of all you have achieved, both in your career and in raising your amazing children and stepchildren. Even if you weren't my brother, I would like to think we would still be friends.
Thank you for your love and support.

NOTE FROM THE AUTHOR

I am a British author and this book has been written using British English. So if you are from somewhere other than the UK, you may find some words spelled differently to how you would spell them. In most cases this is British English, not a spelling mistake. We also have different punctuation rules in the UK.

However if you find any other errors, I would be grateful if you would please contact me helen@helengoldenauthor. co.uk and let me know so I can correct them. Thank you.

For your reference I have included a list of characters in the order they appear, and you can find this at the back of the book.

1

9:18 AM, SATURDAY 13 MARCH

"Oh my giddy aunt," Perry Juke said in a low voice to his friends gathered around the table in the Chasingham House restaurant. "Something's up."

Lady Beatrice, the Countess of Rossex, followed his eyes towards the tall figure of Henry Greenhill, the manager of the prestigious country house, who was standing by the entrance. His usually impeccable dark suit appeared somewhat creased, and his short, well-styled hair seemed less than pristine. Squinting, his eyes darted around the room, betraying an inner turmoil that was wholly out of character for the composed manager.

Perry's right. Something's wrong. Shielding her eyes against the morning sun peeking through the large windows of the restaurant, Bea watched as Greenhill's gaze stopped when it got to their table. Then, with furrowed brows and a tense jaw, he moved towards them, his long strides betraying the urgency of his mission.

"Sorry to disturb you, my lady," Greenhill said in a hushed tone, attempting to keep his voice steady as he gave Bea a small bow. "May I have a word with Chief Inspector

McKeer-Adler, please?" He turned away from the king's niece, his Adam's apple bobbing up and down his neck, and addressed the dark-skinned woman sitting to Bea's right. "In private if you don't mind, chief inspector."

Well, that clinched it. If he was referring to Adler in her official capacity, then there was something serious going on.

Detective Chief Inspector Emma McKeer-Adler from the Protection and Investigations (Royal) Services (PaIRS for short) dabbed her lips with a napkin, then exchanged a quick glance with Perry, who gave a short shrug.

"Yes, of course, Mr Greenhill." She gave them all a brief smile as she rose to join the manager, who had moved to her side. Holding out his arm, he gestured towards the door, and Adler's petite frame glided across the room as she followed him out.

Bea took a sip of her coffee, trying not to stare too blatantly as they left the room.

"What's that all about?" Ellie Gunn flicked her fringe out of her eyes and cast a curious glance towards the disappearing pair.

Claire Beck shook her head, her red glasses slipping down her nose as she leaned forward, her eyes sparkling. "I've no idea, but he looked very flustered. He's normally the epitome of calm. Something's definitely off."

"Indeed." Bea nodded, her green eyes narrowing. *Is it something to do with me?* She hoped not. Adler was here this weekend, along with Ellie, Claire and herself, to celebrate Perry's last weekend as an unmarried man, and she was therefore not on duty. *But if there's a threat to me, will she shift from friend to protector?* Bea felt her pulse quicken, then caught herself. *Don't be so melodramatic, Bea.* She was at a private club in the middle of nowhere in the Cotswolds, where the security was tight and the clientele pre-vetted. *It's unlikely I'm in any danger.*

Glancing around the room, her eyes rested on the only other occupied table in the restaurant, where three women sat. Cammy Redmaine and Flick Spencer, their backs to her, had their heads together, deep in conversation. Mel Parks, sitting opposite, ran her hand through her short swept-back hair as she stared at the door, frowning. There was an empty chair next to her with a half-drunk cup of tea on the table in front of it. *Wasn't Vikki Carrington there the last time I looked?* Bea nudged Perry, who was sitting beside her digging into his full English breakfast. "Did you see Vikki leave? I'm sure she was here earlier."

Perry put his fork down and looked over at the other table. "She was. No, I didn't see her leave. I hope she's okay." He frowned. "Looks like Mercy's not there either."

He was right. A fifth place on the other side of Mel was also empty. Where was Mercy Bright? Bea's heart sank. Was that what Greenhill needed Adler for? Was it something to do with the two women? Her mind raced with possibilities as Bea tapped her fingers on her cup. Should she go over and ask Flick if everything was okay?

The 'birthday girls', as Perry had named them, had arrived at the same time as them yesterday.

Bea had met all the birthday girls except Mercy prior to this weekend as they had all been school friends of Bea's cousin, Lady Caroline Clifford. Felicity 'Flick' Spencer, however, was the one Bea knew best as she was a close friend of Caroline's. Studying Flick in conversation with Cammy, Bea decided they didn't look concerned or worried about anything. She'd best leave it for now.

"Any guesses what Mr Greenhill and Em are discussing?" Ellie whispered, leaning in conspiratorially.

"Perhaps there's been some sort of issue with the hotel," Claire suggested, adjusting her glasses on her nose. "Something has been stolen, or there's a problem with an unruly guest?"

"Us and the birthday girls are the only guests here at the moment," Bea reminded her, nodding at the other table.

"Maybe he's confessing his undying love for her?" Perry suggested with a playful grin, seemingly trying to lighten the mood.

Bea smiled. Whatever was going on, Perry clearly wasn't going to let it dampen the mood of his bachelor weekend. Bea suppressed a sigh. *I have a feeling it might be too late.*

Sensing movement in her peripheral vision, she flicked her gaze towards the door just as Adler appeared. Even from this distance, she could see Adler's face was grim and determined. Bea's heart sank. Whatever it was she was about to tell them, Bea knew it wouldn't be good news.

Adler reached their table and took her seat without a word. She quickly glanced over at the birthday girls' table, then turned back to them. Leaning in, she sighed heavily. "Mercy Bright has been found in her room. She's dead."

THE DAY BEFORE, 11 AM FRIDAY 12 MARCH

The Society Page online article:

Lady Beatrice and Friends Head Off to Chasingham House to Celebrate Her Best Pal's Last Weekend of Freedom

The prestigious private member's hotel and spa, Chasingham House, is hosting a bachelor weekend for Perry Juke (34), best friend of Lady Beatrice (36), the Countess of Rossex, ahead of his wedding to bestselling author and celebrity chef Simon Lattimore (40). The King's niece is believed to have planned the weekend for Mr Juke and three other friends at the sister property to the exclusive The Chasingham Club in Mayfair, London, where the countess is a member. The party will no doubt enjoy exploring the Grade II-listed manor built in 1705, which is surrounded by twenty acres of English countryside in the heart of the Cotswolds. Featuring a formal dining space in The Stables and the renowned cocktail bar, Space, the club also has tennis courts, indoor and outdoor swimming pools, a gym, and extensive spa facilities.

Perry Juke and Simon Lattimore are getting married next weekend at Francis Court, the home of Charles Astley, the sixteenth Duke of Arnwall, and his wife, HRH Princess Helen, the King's sister. Lady Beatrice, who also lives on her parents' Francis Court Estate, owns and manages FC Design and Interiors Ltd along with Mr Juke. The company was commissioned to refurbish and renovate several royal homes and palaces, including Fenn House in Fenshire and, more recently, the King's official residence, Gollingham Palace in Surrey.

Also believed to be staying at Chasingham House this weekend are top models Camile Redmaine (35) and Mel Parks (35), who are celebrating newly-single Cammy's birthday with a group of friends including Felicity 'Flick' Spencer (35), wife of millionaire property developer Barney Spencer (42) and granddaughter of the Earl of Walshaming, and Victoria Carrington (35), the well-known literary agent and recent ex-girlfriend of the American singer and actress, Missie Bradshaw. Mel Parks, on-off girlfriend of Formula One racing driver Justin Reynolds, is the daughter of Andrew Parks (62), who owns both Chasingham House and The Chasingham Club. A little dickie bird tells us Mr Parks is planning to open Chasingham LA in Los Angeles, California, soon having recently secured the freehold on a building in West Hollywood. Mr Parks also owns two nightclubs in Ibiza, Nightlife in New York, and a fine dining restaurant in Monaco called QT.

3

12:30 PM, FRIDAY 12 MARCH

The sunlight streamed through the large bay windows of The Stables at Chasingham House, the private members' hotel and spa nestled in the heart of the Cotswolds, casting a warm golden glow over the elegantly set tables as Perry, Bea, Em, Ellie, and Claire followed Henry Greenhill through the restaurant.

This really is the epitome of luxury and refinement, Bea thought as she gazed around. It reminded her of the Orangery at Francis Court where Perry and Simon were getting married next week. *I just hope the weather will be as nice then as it is today.*

"This will be your table while you're here," the manager told them, indicating a large round table, the crisp white linens and gleaming silverware seeming to sparkle like jewels beneath the ornate chandeliers suspended from the high ceiling. "We only have one other group in residence this weekend, so you will practically have the place to yourselves," he said, smiling. Perry grinned and winked at Bea. *What's he up to?*

The tall man stooped down and pulled a chair out for Bea. "My lady," he murmured.

Bea smiled. "Thank you, Mr Greenhill."

The manager waved his hand over towards a door in the far corner, and a short man smartly dressed in a white shirt, black waistcoat, black tie, and pressed black trousers hurried forward. "This is François. He will look after you." The man stopped and gave a curt bow. Greenhill patted the server on the shoulder, then nodded and left them. François took their drink order, then hurried over to the door he'd come from and disappeared.

"So?" Bea asked Perry as soon as he sat down beside her.

"I know who the other party is," he said triumphantly.

"Oh, who?" Claire cried, hooking her handbag over the back of her chair.

"Well, according to *The Society Page*, Cammy Redmaine and Mel Parks are here for the weekend with some friends. It's Cammy's birthday." Perry crossed his arms and raised an eyebrow as if he knew this through some sort of personal connection to the model.

"As in Cammy, the model?" Ellie asked.

"Supermodel!" Perry corrected. "I can't believe I'm mixing with supermodels this weekend."

Bea suppressed a smile. She would introduce Cammy and Mel to Perry and maybe ask them if they would have a picture taken with him. He would love that.

"Well, we may not be a bunch of supermodels, but don't you dare ditch us for them!" Em said, a half-smile playing on her lips.

"Spoilsport!" Perry pouted, then grinned. "Seriously though, I'm so excited to spend this weekend with you all." Perry, with his short spiky strawberry-blond hair styled to perfection and his blue eyes sparkling with delight, clapped his hands together like he was applauding a particularly spectacular final act of a play.

"Indeed." Bea grinned, glancing around at the sophisticated environment of The Stables. "It will do," she said, dropping her napkin on her jeans.

Adler offered Perry a slow nod. "Yeah, it's not bad," she said, giving a low throaty chuckle.

Claire, her glasses perched on her nose, beamed at Perry as she tucked a stray curl behind her ear. Her brown eyes were alight with excitement as she too scanned the room. "Wow, Perry. This place is amazing."

"I agree!" Ellie said, smiling widely as she shifted in her seat. Her curvy frame, accentuated by the bright-blue, form-fitting dress she wore, showed off her ample bosom and shapely hips. Her long wispy light-brown hair framed her face, and her fringe danced playfully just above her blue eyes. "It gives Francis Court a run for its money." Glancing at Bea, she gasped. "Sorry, my lady. I don't mean it's better," she said, colouring slightly. "It's just that it's…" She trailed off and looked down.

Bea grinned at Francis Court's catering manager. "Ellie, it's okay. You're right. It's beautiful and so light and airy. And please, while we're away from Francis Court and all here as Perry's guests, I'd like it if you called me Beatrice or Bea."

Ellie looked up and returned Bea's grin. "Yes, my lady. I mean, Beatrice."

"And that goes for you too, Claire." Bea turned to the shorter woman.

Francis Court's human resources manager blushed. "Oh, but my lady, it doesn't seem—"

"Claire, please. We're not at Francis Court, and you're not working, so…" Bea hesitated. Maybe Claire felt uncomfortable with that level of familiarity with a member of the royal family and the daughter of her boss. "But I don't want you to feel uncomfortable, so it's up to you." Claire looked at Ellie, then back at Bea before giving a nervous giggle. "Okay."

"And you, Adler. There's no need to be formal around me when you're not working."

Emma McKeer-Adler nodded. "As you wish, Bea. Does that mean you'll stop calling me Adler and start calling me Em?" She raised an eyebrow and gave Bea a cheeky grin.

Touche! "I'll try," Bea said, knowing it would be hard to break the habit.

"Thanks for organising this, Bea," Perry jumped in, smiling. "I could never get into a place like this without your help." He dropped his napkin in his lap.

Bea patted his hand and smiled. "Anything for you, my dear. I thought it would be the perfect spot for us to relax and unwind before your big day!"

He looked around at his friends. "Thank you so much for coming," he said with a beaming smile, his voice filled with genuine warmth.

As they settled into their chairs and perused the menu, Bea couldn't help but feel a spark of anticipation for the weekend ahead. *Good food, good wine, and good company. The perfect combination.*

***

Thirty minutes later, Bea took the last mouthful of her tuna and butter bean salad and pushed her plate to one side. Reaching for her glass of sparkling water, she glimpsed a wistful expression on Em's face. "Is everything all right, Ad...I mean, Em?"

"Yes," Em said wistfully. "I just wish Izzy was here. She would love this room and all the ceramics on display." Em's wife was a ceramic expert, and her job involved restoring period pieces. Bea followed Em's gaze to a tall long cabinet in the corner of the room. It was filled with dinner services of all shapes and sizes, from delicate china painted with gold-and-blue scrolls to intricate hand-painted porcelain plates.

"It looks like something from the late eighteenth century or early nineteenth century," Bea said, having seen many such displays in the state rooms of Francis Court. Em inclined her head, then sighed. Her petite frame slumped slightly in her chair.

"When will Izzy be back from visiting her son in LA?" Perry joined in.

"Wednesday," Em replied, sitting up straight. "Which, by the time we get back from here, will only be a couple of days, I suppose."

"The time will fly by," Bea said sympathetically, her green eyes softening. Em clearly missed her wife. Unexpectedly, Bea's thoughts turned to Richard Fitzwilliam. *I wonder what's he's up to right now?* He was probably sitting in an armchair at Hope Cottage, reading Simon's latest thriller, with soft classical music playing in the background. She smiled to herself. Until recently, she'd not been familiar enough with the detective chief inspector from PaIRS to imagine his spare time activities. But since he'd moved into an empty cottage on the Francis Court estate to recuperate after being shot during a PaIRS investigation a few weeks ago, she'd got to know him a little better.

She, Perry, and Simon had become regular visitors to Fitzwilliam at the cottage, wanting to keep an eye on him as well as keep him company. Simon had been taking over delicious homemade food, while Perry had been bringing him up to date with the gossip he'd read in the trashy magazines he was so fond of. She'd been updating Fitzwilliam on the work she was having done at The Dower House, her old home she'd shared with her late husband James and was now planning to move into with her fourteen-year-old son Sam as soon as it was ready.

She and Fitzwilliam had even ventured out a few times, taking coffee in The Old Stable Block cafe or going on a gentle walk around the gardens of Francis Court. He had been eager to get out of the house, ignoring the warnings from his doctor not to do too much too soon. They had wandered along paths lined with ancient trees that created a natural shelter from the winter sun, talking about their favourite books, TV shows, films, and music or simply admiring the beauty of their surroundings in companionable silence. She had nagged him to rest frequently, and he'd reminded her she was far too quick to tell him what to do, as always. They'd laughed, their past clashes over the murder investigations they'd been involved in together over the last twelve months forgotten.

"Well, at least you'll be able to pamper yourself while we're here," Claire chimed in, dragging Bea away from her musings.

"And at least I've brought you to this oasis of calm," Perry interjected with a grin. "Unlike Simon's poor friends who he's dragged to an adventure centre in the Lake District. Roisin, his best friend, is there making sure they don't get into too much trouble, but it will be a miracle if one of them doesn't break something. They're all big kids, but they forget they're now living in the bodies of middle-aged men!"

Bea joined in the laughter, envisioning Simon navigating

a ropes course or zip-lining through the forest. "Indeed," she agreed. "Well, I, for one, am glad I'm chilling out here instead."

"Hear, hear!" Perry exclaimed, raising a glass of champagne in a toast. The others followed suit, clinking their glasses together.

"We deserve a bit of pampering and relaxation," Ellie said, sipping from her glass.

"Absolutely," Perry agreed, his blue eyes alight with excitement. "And I can't think of a better group of friends to spend this weekend with."

"Have any of you seen the indoor pool yet?" Claire asked. "I've heard it's absolutely stunning."

Bea shook her head. When they'd arrived an hour ago, she'd only had time to unpack, then she'd called Sam at his boarding school to hear about his latest rugby game before she'd headed to lunch.

"Yes," Perry replied, his blue eyes lighting up. "I sneaked a peek at it on my way down. It's quite impressive. Imagine swimming under a glass ceiling that allows in natural light. It looks serene."

"It sounds heavenly," Ellie said, a dreamy look on her face as her red fingernails traced the rim of her champagne flute.

"And I read in the brochure in my room that their sauna is top-notch as well — cedarwood-lined walls and panoramic views of the Cotswolds countryside," Claire added.

"I can't wait for a massage," Em added, her excitement palpable. "After being hunched over my desk all week, I really need one."

"Speaking of treatments," Bea said, a tingle of excitement running up her back. "I can hardly wait for my hot stone massage. I've never had one before, but my cousin, Caroline, says they're incredible for easing tension."

The traumatic events at Gollingham Palace last month had left her with stiffness in her shoulders and neck that needed to be alleviated.

"I'm really looking forward to my body wrap," Ellie declared enthusiastically. "What treatment are you having first, Claire?"

"A facial. I'm hoping it will take years off me," she said, grinning.

"They're great for nourishing and rejuvenating the skin," Ellie told her. "I had one a couple of months ago, and I remember feeling like I'd lost years off my face. What about you, Perry?"

"I'm having a body wrap too," Perry replied, giving Ellie a knowing grin. "They say it can help with toning and firming the skin, and I need that if I'm going to pull off that morning suit I'm wearing next weekend."

"Hey," Claire interjected, looking at her watch. "After we've had dessert, why don't we go for a swim before our treatments? It will be a nice way to start the afternoon."

"Cheers to that," Perry agreed. Clinking their glasses together, they downed their champagne just as François arrived with a selection of mini puddings.

4

1 PM, FRIDAY 12 MARCH

As Bea glanced around The Stables restaurant at Chasingham House, the warm scents of freshly baked bread and roasted vegetables wafted through the air, tempting her taste buds despite her having just finished her dessert. She took a deep breath, inhaling the pleasant aroma and felt a sense of contentment wash over her. She took a sip of coffee, the delicate china clinking softly against the saucer. Across from her, Perry laughed at something Ellie was saying, his eyes crinkling as he grinned. Next to them, Claire was nodding enthusiastically at Em, who was recounting a story, no doubt about her time in PaIRS.

Bea smiled to herself, happy to be sharing a leisurely lunch with this eclectic mix of friends on a sunny Friday afternoon. She let her gaze drift over the restaurant's exposed brick walls and wooden beams, which contrasted beautifully with the crisp white tablecloths and gleaming silverware, when a movement at the entrance caught her eye. The front door swung open and in walked Greenhill, followed by five women.

Bea's table went quiet as even from across the room, the

women's energy was palpable. They glided to their table, led by Camile Redmaine, who was dressed impeccably in a chic floral dress and oversized sunglasses perched on top of her sleek black hair. Vikki Carrington confidently strolled by Cammy's side, a short animal-print dress revealing her long lean legs clad in black boots. Just behind them, Felicity Spencer flicked her long fringe out of her eyes as she turned to say something to Mel Parks, whose modelesque figure was draped in expensive designer clothes, an air of haughty boredom about her.

Bea smiled. *It will be good to catch up with Flick this weekend.*

Bringing up the rear was the only woman Bea didn't recognise. Tall, curvy, and elegant, she seemed slightly over-whelmed by the boisterous group but was forcing an awkward smile onto her face.

Greenhill led them to a large round table on the other side of the restaurant, and the lively conversation and giggles continued as they sat down. Bea wondered what stories or gossip they might be sharing. There was something magnetic about these flashy women that piqued her curiosity.

"That Vikki Carrington certainly has presence, doesn't she?" Ellie said, nodding in the direction of the shortest woman in the group. "Hasn't she just landed the deal for Sir Hewitt Willoughby-Franklin's autobiography?"

Bea smiled wryly. It had been the subject of much discussion recently between her mother Princess Helen and Lady Grace, Sir Hewitt's wife. Her mother thought it was crass that her friend's husband was willingly exposing his family to the public in such a way, but as she had been the one to introduce Lady Grace and Sir Hewitt at a charity ball she'd organised five years ago, she'd agreed through gritted teeth that she could be mentioned in the book but only after Sir Hewitt had promised her final approval of any chapters she would feature in.

"Hasn't she just split with her girlfriend?" Claire asked. They all looked at Perry.

"Well," he said, rubbing his chin. "Yes. From what I read it was Vikki who ended the relationship. Missie is said to be heartbroken." He leaned in and whispered, "Vikki's getting quite the reputation as a serial dater."

Claire and Ellie nodded solemnly as Bea stifled a grimace. Perry was well-known for his voracious appetite for celebrity gossip.

"And," Perry continued in a hushed voice, "did you hear Mel was in a spot of trouble in Ibiza?" Bea rolled her eyes. "It was in the papers," Perry responded defensively, scowling at her. "She got herself into a bit of a mess, and her father had to step in."

"What happened?" Claire asked, her eyes wide.

"Well, apparently, she was over there on a photoshoot, and one of the press who was part of the pack out there followed her back to where she was staying. The next morning, some locals found him in a bush badly beaten and his camera destroyed. He needed hospital treatment. He claimed he'd knocked on the door of Mel's villa, and she'd invited him in. Then he was set upon by two men who beat him up and told him to stay away from Mel, or it would be even worse for him next time."

Claire's mouth dropped open while Ellie shook her head disapprovingly.

Perry continued, "The police arrested Mel, but she denied the whole thing, stating that he made it all up to create a story for his paper. Her father flew over from London and got her out of jail. He's got property over there, so he has quite a bit of sway, I suppose. The next thing you know, they dropped all charges against her." He raised an eyebrow. "Daddy to the rescue."

"Doesn't he own this place?" Ellie asked. Perry gave a nod of agreement.

"It certainly doesn't hurt to have wealthy and influential parents to bail you out when necessary," Claire said with a knowing look.

"True," Perry chuckled. "But it must still be embarrassing for Mel to have her dirty laundry aired in public like that."

"Isn't that the price you pay for being in the public eye?" Em pondered aloud. "Fame always comes at a cost."

Yes, indeed! Bea had had her fair share of being plastered all over the news for as long as she could remember. Leaning back in her seat, she observed the newcomers from afar and wondered what other secrets might lie beneath the surface. She should really go and say hello to Flick. *And it will give me a chance to have a better look at them all.* She rose, and excusing herself from the table, she approached the lively group.

As she neared, Flick caught sight of her and waved enthusiastically. "Beatrice! What a lovely surprise," Flick exclaimed, standing up to greet her.

"Hello, Flick," Bea replied warmly, offering a genuine smile as they hugged. "I saw your party arrive and thought I'd come and say hello."

"Vikki, Cammy, Mel, you all know Lady Beatrice."

"Good to see you all again," Bea said. The women nodded and smiled.

"Mercy, this is Lady Beatrice, the Countess of Rossex." Flick turned to the only person Bea didn't already know. "She's the king's niece. Cammy, Vikki, and I went to school with her cousin, Caroline."

Mercy greeted her politely, her eyes scanning Bea with curiosity and interest.

"This is Mercy Bright, my lady. Her parents are friends of Vikki's parents. She's American." Whether intentional or not, Flick had managed to make it sound like something she needed to apologise to Bea for.

"Nice to meet you, Mercy," Bea said, smiling.

"Are you here celebrating anything special, my lady?" Vikki asked.

"My friend, Perry, is getting married next weekend, so we're here to have some pampering before the madness begins." She paused, then continued, "Well, I won't keep you. Enjoy your lunch, and perhaps we'll catch up in the bar later?"

"Absolutely! We're celebrating Cammy's birthday, so I'm sure we'll be in there for a cocktail or two," Flick replied cheerfully.

Bea tipped her head and smiled before turning and walking back to her table. Now there were more of them, the atmosphere in the restaurant was lively and buzzing with excitement. The sounds of laughter and clinking glasses and the tantalising aromas of delicious dishes being served only heightened the sense of fun and celebration.

"Do you know them?" Perry asked as Bea sat back down next to him. "You didn't say…"

"I know Flick Spencer very well. She's the one with the long brown hair sitting next to Cammy Redmaine. She's a good friend of my cousin, Caroline."

"Ah…" Perry gazed over at the table.

"Did you see the latest photoshoot Cammy and Mel did for *Vogue*?" Claire asked, tapping into her extensive knowledge of the fashion world. "It was absolutely stunning! They were draped in these gorgeous silk gowns, completely owning every pose and angle."

"Ah yes, I saw that one," Perry remarked with a nod. "They make quite the pair, don't they?"

"Totally," Ellie agreed. "I must admit, I've always been fascinated by the world of modelling. The glamour, the travel, the beautiful clothes... It seems like such an exciting life."

"Until someone spills your secrets, that is," Em interjected with a mischievous grin.

Bea began to feel uncomfortable gossiping about the women at the other table. She knew what it was like to have one's actions commented on by other people. When her husband had died in a car accident fifteen years ago with a female passenger beside him, the press speculation had driven her to hide herself away for years. She shot Perry a warning glance, urging him to drop the subject.

"Shall we meet at the pool in ten minutes?" Perry suggested, checking his watch in an exaggerated fashion. "We can fit in a quick dip before our treatments start."

"Indeed," Bea replied, giving him a thankful smile. "I could use some relaxation after that delicious meal."

"Absolutely," Claire chimed in, already gathering her belongings. "I suspect I'll be asleep within ten minutes of them starting my facial!"

"I give you five." Perry grinned as he straightened his suit jacket and rose. "Let's get the pampering started, shall we?"

5

9 PM, FRIDAY 12 MARCH

Bea sank back in the cherry-red plush velvet armchair and took a deep breath. *I think this better be my last cocktail,* she thought, feeling slightly tipsy, yet enjoying the mild buzz in her head. It wasn't like her to overindulge in alcohol, but something about the intoxicating atmosphere of the cocktail bar at Chasingham House encouraged it.

As the soothing music emanating from the speakers in the corners of the room washed over her, her gaze swept around the alcove, taking note of the animated conversations and laughter that filled the air.

Maybe it was the hot stone massage she'd had that afternoon in the Spa, but her limbs were pleasantly heavy as her gaze drifted over to Perry, who was sitting next to Cammy. Cammy, her eyes sparkling, animatedly describing her latest modelling assignment in Croatia. She spoke with such enthusiasm that her cocktail nearly splashed over the rim of her glass. "…and then the photographer said, 'Cammy, darling, if you can't lift your leg any higher than that, then I'll ring my mother because I know she can!'" Cammy exclaimed, causing Perry to chuckle.

"Rude!" Perry said, his face glowing with admiration as he listened in awe to the supermodel.

"So I gave him a high leg that made his eyes water," Cammy replied, her laughter filling the air like tinkling bells.

Across the room, Em sat next to Vikki. They leaned in close, their heads almost touching as they earnestly discussed some matter known only to them. Every now and then, they broke off their conversation to sip their cocktails, their eyebrows furrowing in concentration.

A burst of laughter erupted from the table just beyond them where Claire and Ellie chatted animatedly with Flick and Mel. Claire's hands flailed in the air, punctuating the story she was telling Flick, while Ellie's laughter bubbled up like champagne as she listened to Mel.

Bea smiled. It was great to see how easily Perry's party and the birthday girls had merged into one. The lively chatter and laughter of them all together warmed her heart, but something tugged at the edge of her mind. Her eyes searched the group. Someone was missing…

Mercy. Had she gone up to her room already? It was possible. Mercy had seemed out of place throughout the evening, her presence feeling more like an obligation than a genuine desire to be there. Earlier, Bea had felt sorry for her when she'd noticed that Mercy didn't seem to be interacting with the other girls much. So she had made an effort to talk to her, and they had had a brief conversation about New York — one of Bea's favourite cities and where Mercy had lived prior to her family's move. But although the American had been friendly enough to begin with, she had also been downing cocktails at an alarming rate. As she'd got louder and slightly aggressive with her responses, Bea had excused herself saying she'd needed the bathroom.

Why is she even here? Then she remembered that during a

conversation with Vikki, she'd told Bea how she'd brought Mercy with her only after her mother had nagged her to. Mercy didn't have many friends in the UK, and her parents, friends of Vikki's parents, were worried about her. *Why?* Bea trawled her memory. She couldn't recall that Vikki had elaborated any further. *Was Mercy in some sort of trouble?*

The door to the cocktail bar open, and Mercy, swaying a little, made her way back into the room. Her cheeks were flushed with alcohol, and her eyes seemed unfocused. Bea winced as she watched the woman stumble over an empty chair as she made her way towards her. Steading herself on the back of an armchair next to Bea, she took a glug of her tall red drink, then dropped the glass on the table and collapsed into the chair without a word. All eyes turned to the American.

"Are you alright?" Bea asked softly, leaning across the arm of her chair towards her.

"I'm fine," Mercy snapped, her voice slurred.

Okay, if you say so.

As the conversations around her continued, Bea saw Mel, Flick, Cammy, and Vikki exchange glances, their expressions a mix of embarrassment and pity. It was clear that Mercy's inebriated state hadn't gone unnoticed.

Bea stood up. She needed some water. "I'm going to the bar to get a glass of water. Would you like one too?" she suggested gently. Mercy only grunted in response, her gaze fixed on some indiscernible point across the room. *I'll take that as a yes then.*

Bea made her way slowly towards the other end of the room where Jarvis Freeth, the barman, stood behind the mirrored bar. Tall and handsome in his white shirt and black bow tie, he was like a showman, making the drinks with an almost effortless flair. As she perched on a barstool, she watched in awe as his skilful hands whirled around the glasses and bottles like a master conductor leading an orchestra. As he finished each drink, he set it down on a tray where they sparkled in a riot of colour, waiting for a server to deliver them to the tables.

"Another espresso martini, my lady?" Jarvis asked as he added a sprig of mint with a final flourish to the glass in front of him.

"Thank you, Jarvis, but I believe I've reached my limit for the evening," she replied with a polite smile. "Can I have two large glasses of water with ice, please?"

He nodded and turned away. Bea glanced at her watch. A weariness crept up on her. *Is it too early to suggest a change of pace?* Retreating to a quieter setting and watching a film together as they'd agreed upon earlier sounded rather appealing right now.

6

8:55 AM, SATURDAY 13 MARCH

The scent of freshly brewed coffee mingling with the aroma of sizzling bacon and buttered toast made Bea's stomach rumble as she entered The Stable at Chasingham House for breakfast the next day. The restaurant's warm wood panelling and colourful artwork on the walls created an inviting atmosphere, and she hurried over to the table to join Perry and Em.

She relaxed a bit as she got closer and saw neither Claire nor Ellie had surfaced yet. *I'm not the only one who's late...*

"Sorry I'm late," she said, pulling a chair out and sitting down. "I was so cosy in bed, I couldn't drag myself out of it."

Perry raised an eyebrow. "So it was nothing to do with the numerous cocktails you consumed last night?"

Bea blushed. She wasn't a big drinker and normally preferred a glass of wine to anything else. But the cocktails in the bar last night had been a revelation, and she may have slightly overindulged...

"Coffee or tea, my lady?" François seemed to appear out of nowhere. *Saved by the bell!*

"Coffee please, François." The short, bearded man gave a clipped nod and disappeared.

"Ah, the fashionably late crew has arrived!" Perry quipped, his perfectly styled blond hair catching the soft light filtering through the windows as Claire and Ellie rushed over.

"I'm so sorry. I don't know what was in those drinks last night, but I—"

Perry held up a hand to Ellie, grinning. "Don't worry, everyone seems to have had the same issue." He winked at Bea.

Cheeky!

"I don't think it was the drink," Claire said, taking the seat next to Em. "I think it was the treatments. I'm just so relaxed now, I slept like a log."

"Ah, well, that must be it then." Perry nodded, trying to keep a straight face.

Bea nudged him and whispered, "Behave."

François returned with Bea's coffee, and she took a grateful gulp of the steaming beverage. As the strong, slightly bitter liquid slipped down her throat, it felt like every cell in her body was slowly awakening. *Ah, that's better.*

As the others gave François their breakfast order, Bea glanced up from her cup to see the trio of Flick, Vikki, and Cammy enter the room, a flurry of colour and movement.

Flick, wearing a loose red blouse and skin-tight black jeans, her highlighted brown hair swept back into a messy but stylish bun, walked into the room as if she was gliding on air despite the sky-high heels she had on. Vikki, casual in a baggy green jumpsuit and wedged trainers, still looked totally polished, her chestnut locks tucked behind her ears and cascading down her shoulders. Cammy, taller than the other two, looked every inch the model she was in a white linen shirt tied just above her toned midriff, skinny jeans, and brown suede knee-high boots. *Anyone would think they were about to do a photoshoot*, Bea thought as she looked down at her fitted blue T-shirt and jeans. *Unlike me, who looks like I grabbed the first thing I came across this morning.* Which was exactly what she'd done.

Smiling, Vikki and Cammy waved to them, mouthing, "Good morning," as they made their way to their table across the room, but Flick grinned as she sauntered over to Bea's table, her heavily made-up blue eyes sparkling.

"Good morning, everyone!" she said as she stopped between Perry and Bea. "I don't know about you, but I could've slept all morning."

"Morning, Flick," Bea replied. "We were just saying something similar ourselves." She gave Perry a warning look as he opened his mouth.

"I suspect it was all those amazing cocktails we got through last night," Flick continued.

Perry smirked at Bea.

"We were all done in by eleven," she continued, giving a short laugh as she glanced over at Cammy and Vikki, who were now ordering their drinks. "I used to party all night. I must be getting old! How was your film?"

Bea smiled wryly, recalling how she, Perry, Em, Claire, and Ellie had left the birthday girls in the bar and gone up to Perry's suite, keen to watch a film, and how only she and Perry had made it to the end while the others had gradually dozed off. "Let's just say not everyone saw the whole thing."

"Yes," Perry added with a grin. "My beauty sleep is more important than staying up late these days."

Bea bit back a retort.

"And we were all exhausted from all that relaxing we'd done in the spa," Claire said without a trace of irony.

"Well, we're quite the wild bunch, aren't we?" Flick

sighed dramatically, resting one hand on her hip. "And it's more of the same today for us. Spa, treatments, swimming, cocktails…"

"Us too. It's tough, but someone has to do it." Perry, still grinning, picked up his coffee and took a sip.

"Oh, looks like that's your food," Flick said as François and two other servers appeared through the door by the kitchen, plates piled high with bacon, eggs, toast, tomatoes, and mushrooms. "Right then, back to my wild bunch," Flick said with a laugh. "We'll catch up with you later. Enjoy."

Bea watched her go, noting the way Flick's scrawny frame seemed to command attention despite its slightness. *It looks like she's lost even more weight.* She'd last seen Flick in London about a month ago when Bea had been having coffee with her cousin, Caroline, in Harvey Nichols. Flick had walked in with some girlfriends. She'd come over to say hello and remind Caroline she was waiting for her to reply to a dinner party invitation. What had Caroline said about her when Bea had remarked on how thin Flick looked after she'd left? Something about troubles at home. Was her marriage to Barney Spencer having difficulties? Bea hoped not. She liked the stout and friendly man who played in the same polo team as her older brother Fred. She leaned back in her chair, the pleasant hum of activity punctuated by the occasional *clink* of silverware against china, creating an atmosphere of cozy conviviality. *This is the life…*

"Oh, there's Mel," Ellie said, leaning in conspiratorially as Mel glided into the room. The statuesque model moved with an easy grace, her short blonde-flecked hair swept back and her high cheekbones accentuated by expertly applied make-up. She was dressed impeccably, as always, wearing a tailored dress and heels that wouldn't have looked out of place on a Parisian runway. "Did I tell you what she told me last night?"

Bea's interest was piqued, and she turned her attention back to her friends at the table. Whatever the story was, it promised to be entertaining — and perhaps, just perhaps, it would shed some light on what the reserved model was really like.

"No, do tell," Claire replied, stabbing a tomato and raising it to her lips.

"Well, she—"

"Oh my giddy aunt," Perry interrupted in a low voice, staring at the doorway where Greenhill had just appeared. "Something's up."

———

Perry let out a contented sigh as he bit into his crispy bacon sandwich, then dropping it back on his plate. "She's coming back!" he hissed through his mouthful of food.

Bea, her hand pausing in mid-air as she held her coffee cup, turned to watch Em as she marched towards them. Her grim expression immediately confirmed their earlier speculation that Greenhill had wanted to talk to Em about something serious. A knot formed in her stomach, an uneasy premonition creeping into her thoughts. She exchanged worried glances with Perry as Em reached their table and took her seat without a word.

She quickly glanced over at the other table, then turned back to them. Leaning in, she sighed heavily. "Mercy Bright has been found in her room. She's dead."

A collective gasp rippled through the table, and Claire's fork clattered to the plate, forgotten. Bea's stomach dropped. She was glad she'd not ordered any food. *Please don't let it be murder.* This weekend was supposed to be about Perry… She caught herself. *Bea! Poor Mercy.* She would never see another weekend…

"Dead?" Ellie repeated, her face pale. "But how?"

"I don't know yet. Vikki and Mr Greenhill found her," Em explained, swallowing hard. "He came straight to find me. He said it looked like it might be something she ate or drank that killed her. I'll know more when I go up and look at the body."

Bea stared at Em, trying to process the news. *Was Mercy poisoned?*

Claire covered her mouth with one hand, tears welling in her eyes as she pushed her plate away. "This is dreadful," she choked out. "Poor Mercy."

Bea glanced over at the other table, where Flick and her friends remained blissfully unaware of the tragic news. Flick laughed loudly at something Cammy said, her face now flushed from the exertion. Mel, her head down, was engrossed in something on her phone. All of them were oblivious to the bombshell about to land on them.

Em shifted in her seat. "The local police are on their way," she announced, her voice strained. "In the meantime, I need to go and secure the crime scene and then see if they need me to help out."

"Of course." Perry dipped his head solemnly, his eyes filled with concern. "Will you be okay?"

Em gave him a wry smile. "It's my job." She shrugged, then looking at Bea, added, "And with you being here, my lady, I really need to keep an eye and make sure this is unrelated to your safety."

My lady? Bea stifled a sigh. Em was now in 'Detective Chief Inspector Emma McKerr-Adler from PaIRS' mode. Bea glanced at Perry. *I'm so sorry to spoil your weekend like this.*

He gave her a reassuring smile, then tilted his head at Em. "We get it. Please don't worry."

"But I *am* sorry to have to leave you like this. Carry on without me and try to enjoy the rest of the day. I'll catch you all later."

"Be careful," Claire said softly, reaching out to give Em's hand, still resting on the table, a reassuring squeeze.

"Oh, and take some photos of the crime scene, will you? Simon likes…" Perry trailed off when he caught sight of Bea's face.

What's he doing? We don't want to get involved in the investigation of a crime. This is a weekend of pampering. But then again, poor Em. Her weekend was unlikely to be the relaxing one she'd expected. "Please let us know if there's anything we can do to help you, chief inspector," Bea said with a smile. Em nodded and rose.

Bea glanced over again at Flick's table, where Flick and Cammy were still chatting. How long before they would learn of Mercy's death? Would they be upset or merely sad for someone they didn't really know? A shiver ran down her spine. Or had one of them wanted her dead? *Don't be silly, Bea. It was most probably an accident.* She mustn't let the last twelve months, when she'd been unlucky enough to get caught up in several murders, cloud her judgement. *Murder is rare.*

"Will you inform the others?" Ellie said softly, her eyes also drifting towards Flick, Cammy, and Mel.

Em tilted her head towards them. "I'll make sure someone tells them soon. In the meantime, let's give them a few more moments of peace, shall we?"

Bea bowed her head in agreement, her heart heavy with sorrow. "They'll find out soon enough," she muttered.

"Thanks all of you," Em murmured before hurriedly

making her way towards the exit, her shoulders hunched as if trying to fend off the chill that had descended upon the room. Bea's gaze moved back to the other table and fell on Mel, whose eyes followed Em as she left the room. She seemed to be uneasy. *Has Mel guessed something is up?* Bea stifled a shudder. The restaurant, which had once felt so cozy and welcoming, was now tainted by the shadow of death. Bea glanced back around her table, noting the shock etched on the faces of her friends.

"Do you think someone killed her?" Claire whispered, her fingers absently tracing the rim of her teacup, her gaze distant.

"Hard to say," Perry replied, his expression pained. "I got the impression no one here knew Mercy well except, maybe, for Vikki. She seemed very…guarded to me."

"True," Ellie joined in, her brow furrowed in thought. "But someone must have known her well enough to want her dead."

Bea shuddered. A killer could be lurking among them. She looked towards the other table — perhaps even someone she considered a friend. *Bea! Stop. It's too early to be making outlandish assumptions.*

"Maybe it was someone from her past," Perry suggested, his blue eyes sparkling. "Someone who followed her here."

"Or maybe it was something that happened during her time here," Ellie countered, her eyes scanning the room as if searching for a hidden threat. "She might have stumbled onto something she wasn't supposed to see."

"Either way, it's terrifying to think someone in this peaceful place could be capable of murder," Claire murmured, her voice barely audible.

"Stop!" Bea whispered urgently. "We don't even know

she *was* murdered. It could have been an accident, or she could have died of natural causes."

"Bea's right," Perry agreed, a grim expression settling on his face. "We shouldn't get too carried away. We'll find out more later."

"And until then," Bea said determinedly, "we'll stick together and carry on with our plans to enjoy being pampered."

As they returned to their breakfast, each of them couldn't help but cast furtive glances at the table in the corner. A pervasive air of unease had replaced the festive atmosphere of earlier. Bea's chest tightened with sympathy for Flick, Cammy, and Mel as they braced themselves for the terrible truth that was about to shatter their morning.

7

9:22 AM, SATURDAY 13 MARCH

Walking along the corridor of the third floor of Chasingham House, Detective Chief Inspector Emma McKeer-Adler looked down at her grey tracksuit and black trainers. *Should I have gone back to my room and changed first?* It felt unprofessional to be investigating an unexplained death dressed as if she was about to play a game of basketball. She paused and reminded herself she wasn't officially investigating anything at the moment. She was in a caretaker role until they appointed someone locally. Unless the initial assessment showed Lady Beatrice was in any danger, she would probably be told by her boss Superintendent Blake to do nothing more than keep a watching brief on what the local lads were up to while Bea was still on-site.

As Em rounded the corner, two figures were hovering outside the door of a room halfway along the corridor. Henry Greenhill and Vikki Carrington looked up as she approached, their faces etched with worry and disbelief.

The tall manager of Chasingham House stepped forward to greet her. "Detective chief inspector, thank you so much for doing this. The latest from the local police is that they are still trying to find someone to attend." He shook his head, his disapproval palatable. "There's been some sort of trouble in Cirencester, apparently, and all their senior officers are involved." Em knew from her boss that the "some sort of trouble" was in fact a complicated large-scale raid on a likely cannabis farm just outside the Cotswolds town. She sympathised with the local CID. It was just bad timing.

"I'm sure they'll get here as soon as they can, Mr Greenhill," she told him, then turned to a pale-looking Vikki standing beside him.

"You're the police?" Vikki asked, a frown creasing her forehead.

Didn't she already know that? Em tried to recall her conversation with Vikki last night when the two parties had joined each other over cocktails. They had chatted about many things — from their experience of being gay women in society to what books they read, but now she came to think about it, her job hadn't come up. "I work for the Protection and Investigation (Royal) Services. We're a division of City Police."

"So you're here protecting Lady Beatrice?" Vikki asked, her brown eyes curious. "I just assumed you were one of Perry's friends."

"I am. I'm off duty. And Lady Beatrice is here in a private capacity." She shrugged. "But someone needs to secure the crime scene, and the local guys aren't here yet, so Mr Greenhill asked me to help."

Vikki bobbed her head, her long hair falling over her face. She tucked it behind her ears and gave Em a nervous smile. "Sorry. It was just a surprise, you know?"

"Of course," Em said, giving her a reassuring smile. "Are you okay? I know it's hard finding a dead body, especially when it's someone you know."

Vikki sighed and pushed her hands into the pockets of her baggy jumpsuit. "It's been a huge shock. I won't lie. But I'm fine now, thanks. I didn't really know her that well, anyway."

Something about the way Vikki had dismissed her relationship with Mercy caught Em's attention. *And you didn't like her much, did you?* Now wasn't the time, but she would come back to that later. "I just have a couple of questions for you both, then you can go. Can you tell me what happened this morning, please?"

The hotel manager turned to Vikki, and she nodded. "When Mercy didn't come down to breakfast and she didn't answer her phone, I assumed she'd overslept. But then I got a bit worried. It wasn't like Mercy to be late for anything and particularly not for food. When I told the others, Mel suggested we ask one of the hotel staff to check on her." She turned to Greenhill.

"I was in the lobby, and I saw Miss Carrington heading to reception. I asked her if anything was amiss. She told me of her concerns for her friend, and as my staff were busy, I offered to accompany her to Ms Bright's room. We knocked on the door and called her name." He paused and swallowed loudly. "When we got no reply, I used my master key to enter the room and found..." He trailed off and stared at the closed door with 303 on it in big brass numbers.

"And did you both go into the room?"

"Yes," Vikki replied, her voice wavering slightly. "I just thought we'd find her asleep in bed, but..." She looked down at the floor as if unable to finish the sentence.

"Did either of you touch anything?"

"I bent down and checked for a pulse, but I knew it was pointless. She looked like she'd been dead for a while," Greenhill replied.

"But apart from that?"

They both shook their head.

"Okay, thank you. That will be all for now, although no doubt the investigating officer will have more questions." *What else?* Her mind raced to organise a plan of action. *Get a space for the investigation team. Tell the others. Find Mercy's family.* "In the meantime, Vikki, I will need Mercy's next of kin details, please."

Vikki straightened up and jerked her chin in agreement. "She was living with her parents in Chelsea. Her father works at the American embassy. I'll ring my parents and get the number for you."

"Thank you. And Mr Greenhill, I need you to arrange some rooms for the police to use as interview spaces and an incident room while they investigate."

"Of course, chief inspector."

Don't let anyone leave.

"Oh, and Mr Greenhill. Everyone must stay on-site until the police say otherwise. That's staff and guests. So can you make sure no one leaves, please?"

He bobbed his head, then he and Vikki headed off down the corridor.

Em's thoughts turned inwards, trying to anticipate the challenges that lay ahead in this investigation. Had it been an accident? Or something more sinister? She knew that was the first thing she...*they* would need to establish.

"Time to get to work," she muttered under her breath, her expression set with determination as she opened the door to Mercy's room.

———

Em stepped into the dimly lit bedroom, her eyes immediately scanning the surroundings for any signs of a disturbance. The room was tastefully decorated with a mix of vintage and modern furniture — a testament to Chasingham House's unique charm, with soft rose walls adorned with watercolour paintings of idyllic English countryside scenes. Along the wall, dominating the room, was a luxurious four-poster bed draped in pale lavender linens. Not slept in, Em noted, as her eyes were drawn to the lifeless body of a curvy woman in a short gold evening dress lying on the floor by the side of the bed nearest to her. Mercy Bright. Em's heart clenched at the sight.

Mercy had one hand on the floor just out of reach of a mobile phone lying in front of her, the other raised to her throat as if desperately trying to claw out some unseen assailant. Her eyes were wide with shock and fear. There was dried vomit around her mouth. Em took a deep breath, pushing away the wave of emotion threatening to overwhelm her. It never got any easier to see someone whose life had been cut short.

"Focus, Em," she whispered to herself as she opened the PaIRS app she used to record all investigations, then began snapping pictures of the scene with her phone. After taking photos of the body from various angles, she started on the room. There was a small pile of jewellery on the bedside table — two diamond rings, a chunky gold necklace, and a bracelet. They were expensive-looking pieces. Clearly this hadn't been a robbery gone wrong.

Em moved around the bed. There was a large designer handbag on the other side by the bedside table. It was open. She peered inside but saw nothing of interest. She took a picture anyway, then walked over to the table by the window. There was a tall empty glass on its top, its contents long gone. Em recognised the glass as one of the ones from the cocktail bar. Had Mercy brought a drink up with her? She took a photo of the glass. She'd have to ask the bartender if he recognised it. What was his name? *Jeff? No, not Jeff. Maybe —*

"DCI McKeer-Adler?"

Em spun around as a tall dark-skinned man sporting a well-trimmed goatee walked into the room, followed by a short slightly chubby woman carrying a bag. "I'm DS Victor Meed." He held out his hand, smiling. "Please call me Vic."

"Hi, Vic," Em said, returning the sergeant's smile and handshake.

"And this is Doctor Romaine."

The woman gave a quick nod and headed straight for the body on the floor by the bed.

Em and the sergeant followed her.

"Sorry we're so late getting here, ma'am," the younger man said apologetically. "We have the whole of CID tied up with this raid, and—"

Em held up her hand. "There's no need to apologise, sergeant. I know how much manpower is required to pull off something of that size," she said, giving him a brief smile. "So, I haven't touched anything," she told him. "But—" She suppressed a smile when she recalled Perry's earlier request. "I've taken a few photos just so we have a record if we need it before your forensic team gets here. I thought—"

The shrill ring of a phone pierced the sombre atmosphere. DS Meed mouthed, "Sorry," as he fished his mobile from his pocket and answered it, nodding seriously as he listened.

Simultaneously, Em's own phone buzzed with an incoming text. Glancing down, she read the message from her boss.

. . .

Superintendent Blake (PaIRS): *Local CID should be there soon. A DCI Alan Rivers will take over. Handover what you have and enjoy the rest of your weekend.*

Em took a deep breath. A mixture of irritation and relief washed over her. Someone else would deal with this now. She could continue celebrating Perry's last weekend as a free man. Would this DCI Alan Rivers get to the bottom of Mercy's death? She glanced down at the body. Could she really walk away from this now?

8

9:40 AM, SATURDAY 13 MARCH

"Looks like DCI Rivers will be here soon," DS Meed said, ending his call and looking over at Em. His eyes met hers, then he rapidly looked away. What was that she'd seen on his face? Resignation? *This doesn't bode well.*

"It appears so," she replied. "But in the meantime, let's continue, shall we?" Already, she was mentally compiling a list of questions she wanted to ask. But how many would she get to before Rivers appeared? Well, first they needed to know if Mercy had died accidentally or if they were looking for a murderer. "What can you tell us, doctor?" she asked, addressing the woman kneeling next to Mercy's body on the floor by the bed.

Doctor Romaine looked up from her examination. "From my initial assessment, I'd say death occurred over eight hours ago," she said, her voice steady despite the distressing sight. "The vomit suggests it could be poison or a reaction to something; we'll need to run some tests to be certain."

Over eight hours ago. That was consistent with Mercy still being in her party clothes and the bed undisturbed. She looked over at the empty glass on the table. "Could it be from something she drank?"

The doctor nodded. "Possibly."

"There's no sign of any food in the room, but that glass is empty." She pointed out to Meed. "We need to get that checked." He bobbed his head.

She turned back to the doctor. "You say over eight hours. Can you be any more specific?"

The doctor adjusted her round glasses, pausing for a moment before continuing, "You see, chief inspector, the rate of cooling can help us determine the time of death more accurately," she explained, her voice carrying an air of authority.

"Go on," Em said, her eyes narrowing as she listened intently. *But make it quick. Rivers might be here any moment.* In her experience, doctors could ramble on for hours about body temperatures and rigor mortis. She just wanted a more accurate time.

"Once a person dies, their body slowly cools down until it reaches the ambient temperature of the room," the doctor continued, gesturing around the bedroom. "However, this process isn't uniform. For example, internal organs retain warmth longer than the skin or extremities."

Em looked at Mercy's lifeless form, noting the pale, cold-looking skin on her outstretched hand.

"Rigor mortis is another factor we consider when determining the time of death," the doctor went on, as if giving a lecture to a group of students. "That's the stiffening of the body after death due to chemical changes in the muscles."

Yes, I know! This wasn't her first rodeo. She smiled, knowing a response would only prolong the explanation.

"Typically, rigor mortis begins within two to six hours after death and lasts for approximately eighteen to thirty-six hours," the doctor said. "It then dissipates as the body continues to break down."

Nice! A chill ran down Em's spine. Had Mercy suffered? Looking down at the clawed hand, she feared so. "So based on your assessment, how far along is Mercy in the process?" she asked, her voice steady despite the wretched thoughts in her head.

The woman scrambled up and rubbed her chin. "Judging by the stiffness of her limbs and the overall body temperature, I'd say she's been dead roughly eleven hours."

"Thank you, doctor," Em said, giving the woman a grateful smile. She turned to Meed. "So that would place her time of death around eleven o'clock last night."

"Obviously, I'll know more when I get the body back to the lab for a thorough examination. I'll get my report completed as soon as I can." The woman picked up her bag and headed for the door. As she reached it, the door opened, and she stepped aside as the forensic team entered the room. Clad in their sterile overalls and masks, they resembled a group of extra-terrestrial visitors. The doctor said something to one of them, pointing to Mercy's body, then left the room.

"Morning, Meed," the lead forensic officer greeted. "We're here to give this place the once-over."

Meed turned to Em. "This is DCI McKeer-Adler from PaIRS. She's in charge of the investigation until DCI Rivers arrives."

The man hesitated enough for Em to clock his raised eyebrow, then nodded. "Ma'am. Where would you like us to start?"

She gestured towards Mercy's body. "Please start with the immediate area around the body, then work your way outwards. The doc thinks she may have been poisoned or had a reaction to something she ate or, more likely, drank. There's an empty glass on the table over there. Take it back to the lab for analysis. I'd like to know what exactly was in that glass."

As the team set to work, Em turned to Meed. "Can you compile a list of everyone — staff and guests who were at the hotel last night so we can use it for cross-referencing and ruling out suspects? The manager's name is Henry Greenhill. He'll be able to help you with that." Meed gave a short nod. "Also find out if they have any CCTV in the building. Then we need to interview everyone. So let's—"

"It's okay, chief inspector. I'll take over from here."

Em looked up and found herself face to face with a bald man of about fifty who was only a few inches taller than her.

"Detective Chief Inspector Alan Rivers from Chase CID." He held out his hand.

Em took it, trying not to recoil when her hand found itself in a clammy grip.

Meed stepped forward. "We were just—"

Rivers held up his hand, and Meed fell silent. "I'm here now, sergeant, so I'll decide what you do next. Understand?"

Rude!

"Yes, sir." Meed's head dropped, and he took a step backwards.

That was so uncalled for...

Rivers gave an almost imperceptible smile before turning back to Em.

Smug so-and-so.

"Now, chief inspector, if that's all?"

Em frowned. *Is he dismissing me?* "Don't you want me to bring you up to date—"

The hand came up again. Em's hackles rose. She stared at the man with the large bulbous nose holding up his black-rimmed glasses. She wanted to punch it.

"I caught up with the doc just as she was leaving. I know

the time of death is about eleven last night, cause yet to be determined, but it seems most likely an accidental death."

Had that really been what Doctor Romaine had said? That hadn't been the impression she'd given Em.

"So," Rivers continued, "I'm happy I can take it from here."

His gaze flickered around the scene, then rested on Mercy's body before glancing away. His reactions seemed to be those of someone who'd seen it all before and was bored with it by now. "I'm sure your charge will wonder where you are." There was a sarcastic edge to his voice, and Em clenched her jaw.

Be professional. Don't let the idiot get to you. She'd come across a similar attitude from police officers outside of London before. They seemed to think being an officer in PaIRS was some sort of glorified babysitting role for the royal family. A sharp twinge in her leg reminded her of how it had recently been smashed up in a failed attempt to kidnap the king's brother. People like Rivers had no idea of the danger PaIRS officers put themselves in to perform their duties. *He's not worth it.* "Very well. I'll leave you to it, chief inspector. If you need any—"

"I'll need to interview you and your party, of course, to find out where you all were at the time of this woman's death."

This woman? She gave him an icy stare. "Her name is Mercy Bright."

"Yes, yes." He waved his hand as he turned and moved towards the window. "Please join the others. I'll come and address everyone when I've finished up here."

Biting her tongue, Em gave the back of the man dressed in a dark shirt, chinos, and tweed jacket an evil look. Just as she swivelled round, she caught Meed's gaze and saw the embarrassment in his eyes. She gave him a sympathetic smile before turning on her heel and stomping out of the room, her fists clenched tightly at her sides. She had a bad feeling Rivers was going to cling to this idea of an accidental death just because it offered the easiest way out. Well, she wouldn't let him. If Mercy Bright had been murdered, she would find out who by whether Rivers liked it or not!

9

MEANWHILE, SATURDAY 13 MARCH

Her fingers idly tracing the intricate patterns on the fine china side plate before her, Bea glanced around The Stable as the others chatted nervously amongst themselves. They had been asked to stay in the restaurant by Mr Greenhill. He and Vikki had come into the room ten minutes ago, both looking sombre. While Vikki had hurried over to join her friends at the table on the other side of the room, Henry had stopped a few metres inside, his dark eyes tight with concern.

Bea quickly glanced over at the other table. Cammy, Flick, and Mel were huddled around Vikki, who was whispering to them earnestly. *Is she telling them Mercy's dead?* Flick gasped and placed her hand over her mouth as Vikki patted her arm. Cammy slowly shook her head while Mel ran her fingers through her short hair. *That answers that question!* Bea frowned. Should Vikki be telling them? Wasn't that a job for the police? *Hold on though. This isn't necessarily murder,* she reminded herself.

Greenhill cleared his throat. "Excuse me, everyone," he said, his voice strained yet still commanding their attention. "I'm afraid there has been a serious incident upstairs, and the police are on-site. They have asked me to request that you all remain here in this room until they're able to talk to you. This is a difficult situation, and I'm very sorry for the inconvenience this may cause you. My staff will continue to serve you food and drink if you require it, and I'm sure you won't be kept any longer than is necessary. Thank you."

Bea smiled to herself; 'difficult' was a rather gentle way to describe it. *Poor Mr Greenhill.* Even though it wasn't his fault, from what she'd observed of the man, he was the type of manager who would feel responsible that his guests were now having their relaxing weekend ruined on his watch. She glanced over at him standing by the exit, his arms clasped in front of him. He looked like a very upmarket bouncer.

There was no question — Mercy's shocking death had cast an uneasy pall over the room that seemed to hang in the air like heavy smoke. Bea tried to focus on something else, anything to distract herself from the questions swirling around in her mind. Her gaze settled on the gleaming silverware, each piece polished to perfection. How exactly had Mercy died? Were there any clues? What time had it happened? And, of course, the key question — had it been murder?

"I wonder how long they'll be." Claire leaned into the middle of the table and hissed, "I need to go to the loo."

"I'm sure they won't be long," Ellie said gently, placing a comforting hand on Claire's arm. "Can you wait a little while?"

Claire bobbed her head, looking down at her half-full tea cup. "I wish I hadn't drunk so much tea."

"More coffee?" Perry whispered to Bea, his voice a welcome distraction from the subdued atmosphere. She nodded gratefully. He lifted the coffeepot, and she held out her cup, allowing him to pour the steaming liquid into it. She took a sip, the warmth filling her from within, providing a small fleeting comfort amid the drama.

"Thank you." She gave Perry a weak smile. He returned it but looked uneasy. They weren't used to being on the outside of an investigation, and not knowing what was going on was clearly frustrating him as much as it was her. *Where's Em?* Would she tell them everything she knew, or would she stay in professional mode and not share any details?

Bea's only prior experience of working with Em had been during their last case when, along with DCI Richard Fitzwilliam, they'd solved two murders and had found out once and for all the truth behind Bea's husband's death. She suppressed a sigh. If Em was anything like Fitzwilliam, who Em had worked with on the initial investigation into the earl's fatal car accident fifteen years ago, then she wouldn't want Bea and Perry to interfere with police business.

Bea's gaze shifted to the other table, where Vikki sat surrounded by Flick, Mel, and Cammy. The atmosphere at their table now seemed heavy with a mixture of shock and disbelief.

Flick nervously twirled a strand of her highlighted hair around her finger, her usually animated features shadowed with unease. She darted a glance at Vikki, who gave her a reassuring smile. Mel leaned back in her chair, her statuesque posture somehow making her seem even more untouchable than usual. Her blue eyes held a faraway look, as if she were mentally distancing herself from the situation. And then there was Cammy, her stylish glasses perched on her nose, her fingers drumming an anxious rhythm on the table.

The door opened, and Em entered. Head down, she hurried over. Pulling out a chair, she flopped into it, her face flushed as she grabbed a pot from the middle of the table and sloshed black coffee into the cup in front of it. She gulped down half the cup in one go, then slowly put it down and met their inquisitive stares.

"Are you okay?" Perry asked.

Em let out a long sigh. "Chief Inspector Rivers from Chase Police has just arrived," she said through gritted teeth. "And he's a complete ar—"

"Does that mean you're not investigating Mercy's death?" Claire jumped in, her eyes shining.

"Yes, we were hoping you would give us the inside track," Ellie added.

"Well, Rivers has made it *very* clear he doesn't need my help," Em replied, downing the rest of her coffee.

Bea frowned. But surely PaIRS outranked the local CID? It certainly had in every case she'd been involved in so far. "I thought if there was a crime involving the royal family, then PaIRS had seniority?"

Emma rocked her head from side to side while shrugging. "It's not that simple, I'm afraid. If the crime takes place on royal premises, then yes, we're automatically in charge. And with places like Francis Court, we have an arrangement with Fenshire CID that we have jurisdiction. But anywhere else, unless there's a direct threat to a member of the royal family or something that could be interpreted as a threat, then we're on dodgy ground. It all depends on the local force. If Mercy's death turns out to be murder, then they're obliged to keep PaIRS in the loop, but at the moment, as no crime has been proven to have been committed, if Rivers doesn't want me on the case, then I have no choice but to step aside."

Bea studied Em's face. Her eyes were narrowed, and her lips were pressed together in a thin line. Her body was tense; she looked ready to burst out of her chair. *Oh dear, this Rivers chap has really upset her.*

"That's a shame," Perry said. "We even thought we could help you…" He trailed off, disappointment in his voice.

Bea's eyes met Em's, and she saw something else too. Determination. It was as if Em had made up her mind about something and wasn't going to be swayed from it.

Bea leaned in. "But you're going to investigate anyway, aren't you?" she whispered.

Em looked towards the door, then back at their expectant faces. She nodded. "But I can't do it alone, so I'll need your help."

Bea blinked. *We're going to investigate Mercy's death?* She swallowed. *And behind the police's back?* She glanced at Perry, who was trying unsuccessfully to suppress a broad grin. Well, there was no doubt he was up for it. *But it's supposed to be our weekend to relax.* His flashing eyes told her he would rather investigate a murder. Ellie and Claire seemed equally enthralled. *Well, if you can't beat them…* She smiled at Em. "Of course we'll help."

Just then, two men walked into the room. The shorter one, dressed as if he'd just come from an audition for the part of 'bad guy number two' in a cheap thriller movie, cleared his throat. "Ladies, can I have your attention, please?" *He must be DCI Rivers.* The room went quiet, his authoritative voice drawing everyone's attention. The taller man, dressed in a black suit and crisp white shirt, stood behind Rivers, his eyes downcast.

"Thank you all for waiting," Rivers began, his voice clear and steady. "I'm Detective Chief Inspector Rivers from Chase CID, and this"—he gestured over his shoulder with his thumb —"is Detective Sergeant Meed. As you probably know, a guest, Mercy Bright, was found dead in her room this morning. As we're unable to establish the cause of death at this time, DS Meed and I will need to talk to all the guests and staff to establish Mrs Bright's last known movements and anything else that may throw light on what might have happened."

As he addressed the room, Bea looked over to study the reactions on those at the other table. Flick was nervously biting her lip, her eyes darting towards Vikki, who was sitting next to her. *What's she so worried about?* Mel looked like she was maintaining her normal composed demeanour, but Bea could make out a small tic below her eye that suggested she was not as unconcerned about Mercy's death as she made out. Cammy's fingers had ceased their drumming. Her expression was guarded as she regarded the two police officers. Then, suddenly, her eyes widened, and she looked at the others. *Has she just realised Mercy's death might not be an accident or has something else caused that reaction?*

"Please remain here while we call you in one by one. After we've spoken to you, you can go about your business but kindly remain on-site," Rivers instructed, his deep voice resonating throughout the room. "We appreciate your cooperation." He and Meed had a whispered conversation, then the chief inspector left the room, and Meed headed towards the other table. He said something to Vikki. She dipped her head in acknowledgment, then got up and followed him out of the room.

There was a momentary silence, then Em cleared her throat and turned to Perry. "I'm so sorry to ruin your weekend. If you want me to leave it to that—" She rubbed her forehead as if she was in pain. "Er, man. Then, of course, I will respect your wishes. It's your weekend after all."

Perry reached out and squeezed her hand. "Investigating a potential murder is much more exciting than a facial any day. So you don't need to apologise, Em." Then he grinned.

"Unless, of course, you killed her. Then you really would owe me an apology for disrupting my weekend."

Em's shoulders relaxed, and she grinned back. Bea smiled. Trust Perry to know how to break the tension. Em leaned in. "So are we all in?" she asked in a hushed tone, looking around the table. Everyone nodded in agreement. "Great. So they're going to question us all now to find out about our movements last night. Once they've finished, we should all be free to do what we want."

Claire let out a loud sigh of relief. "Great, cause I really need the loo."

Em smiled at her, then continued, "I suggest we meet up in Perry's suite." She looked at Perry, and he nodded enthusiastically. "Then we can decide on a plan of attack." They all nodded again. "In the meantime, let me tell you what I know so far..."

10:30 AM, SATURDAY 13 MARCH

"Please sit down, Lady Rossex." DCI Rivers gestured towards a set of plush chairs and a sofa arranged around a low coffee table in the Garden Room at Chasingham House. Bea sank into an armchair and looked at the sunlight streaming through the floor-to-ceiling windows, casting a warm glow on the polished wooden floor. The scent of roses lingered in the air from the elegant flower arrangements dotted around the room.

"I need to ask you a question about where you were last night."

Bea gave a curt nod as DS Meed stepped forward and placed a small recording device on the table in front of her. *Maybe they don't have an app like the PaIRS officers use?* She smiled, remembering the murder they'd investigated at Drew Castle at the beginning of this year and how, when forced to use the 'new-fangled' recording tool that was linked directly to their PaIRS systems, Fitzwilliam had told her how he much preferred his trusty notebook and pen.

"So, Lady Beatrice, please can you tell me where you were last night between ten and midnight?"

Bea's eyes sprang open, and her brain seemed to freeze for a second. Was she being asked to provide an alibi? She looked at Rivers. He nodded slowly, smirking. Was he enjoying the situation she was in? *Oh, no. Is he one of those people who doesn't like the royal family and loves to see us squirm?* "Er, we left the bar at about ten—"

"We being who?"

"Oh, er…me, Perry Juke, Claire Becks, Ellie Gunn, and Em…I mean Detective Chief Inspector McKeer-Adler."

"So you're on first-name terms with your protection detail, are you?" he asked, a sneer in his voice.

Yep, he's definitely not a royalist! She raised her chin. "DCI McKeer-Adler is not here babysitting me, chief inspector, if that's what you think. She's off duty. I'm here in a private capacity with a group of friends having a relaxing weekend with Mr Juke before he gets married. She is also a friend of Mr Juke's. That's why she's here."

DS Meed coughed, and Bea looked up to see him with his hand over his mouth, his eyes shining.

Rivers crossed his arms. "Well, thank you for clarifying that, my lady." *He doesn't look very thankful.* "And then where did you go?"

"We went to Perry's suite on the first floor. We stayed there and watched a film, which finished just after midnight, then we said goodbye to Perry and left."

"What, all of you?"

"Yes, all five of us were together."

Was that a look of disappointment on his face? *I bet he'd love it if me or Em didn't have an alibi for eleven.*

"Did anyone leave Mr Juke's suite during that time?"

Bea shook her head firmly. "No."

"And can you confirm where your room is, please?"

"Yes. We're all on the first floor. I'm next door to Perry.

Claire is next door to me. Ellie is opposite Claire, and Emma's next to Ellie."

"Thank you. And did you meet the victim before yesterday?"

The victim? *Does that mean he thinks she was killed?* His face was disinterested. Like this was just his job. Something he did every day. No emotion; just get the job done. *No, I just bet that's how he refers to anyone who's died.*

"Mercy Bright?" she asked innocently. *The poor girl deserves to be called by her name. She was a person, not just a statistic.*

"Er, yes." Rivers unfolded his arms and leaned forward in his chair. "Did you know her?"

"No, sorry, chief inspector," Bea said. "I'd never met her before yesterday."

"And did you talk to her at all yesterday? Was she acting normally?"

"I had a brief conversation with her about New York. That's where she lived before she came over here with her parents, but apart from that..." Bea shrugged.

Rivers sighed. "And when did you last see her?" he asked wearily.

"When we left the bar at about ten, she was still there with the others."

Rivers rose. "Well, that's all for now, Lady Rossex. You're free to go, but please remain on-site in case we have any more questions."

Bea stood. "Yes, of course."

"And thank you for your help, my lady," Meed said quickly as he leaned down and switched off the tape recorder.

Rivers gave him a dirty look.

Bea smiled at the young man. "My pleasure, sergeant," she said as she turned and left the Garden Room.

11

11 AM, SATURDAY 13 MARCH

"So now that we're all done with being questioned," Em said, moving her wireless mouse, and watching her laptop screen come to life. "I've been thinking about how best to tackle this." She pulled the machine towards her on the desk in Perry's hotel suite and sat down in the leather swivel chair in front of it.

"Indeed," Bea said, her eyes roaming around the room. Ellie and Claire were lounging on two oversized sofas in the spacious living room next to the two armchairs she and Perry occupied. Above a marble fireplace to Bea's left, a large flat-screen television hung on the wall. Two tall antique wooden cabinets with glass doors stood on either side of the fireplace. One was filled with crystal decanters, glittering glasses, and a large selection of miniature bottles of wines, spirits, and cans of beer. The other was half-filled with books, with a note propped up on the inside of the glass, encouraging guest to help themselves. To one side of the room was a large work space, where Em was busy typing.

Last night, despite the height of the room, it had felt cozy while they'd been watching a film. Now, with the huge navy-blue striped curtains pulled back, the room was spacious and well-lit, with a beautiful view of the oak-lined driveway leading to the hotel's entrance. A warm glow from the low winter sun lit up the other side of the room where two doors led to the bedroom, dressing room, and bathroom. *This is so much bigger than my room!* She smiled. Perry certainly deserved the best room in the hotel on his special weekend. And, of course, now that it was doubling up as their operations room, it was really handy.

"So what do you want us to do?" Perry asked.

Em spun her chair around to face them. "I know you and Bea have helped Fitz in the past—"

Bea stifled a laugh. *Helped? I'm not sure that's how Fitzwilliam would describe it!* How many times over the last year had he told them to stop interfering and leave the investigating to the police?

"—and, according to him, you're both extremely observant and have a way of getting information out of people—"

She could just imagine Fitzwilliam telling Em that with a scowl on his face, in a voice laced with disapproval. He'd always been miffed that people would tell her and Perry things they wouldn't tell the police.

"—so I could do with that right now." Em met Bea's eyes. "He also told me you have really good instincts, Bea."

Really? Fitzwilliam said that? He'd teased her about her 'woman's intuition', as he called it, during past cases. A warmth spread through her. *He thinks I have good instincts...*

"And Perry," Em continued, "he said you're excellent at getting people to open up to you."

Perry puffed out his chest. "Well, I don't like to brag, but..."

Em smiled, then turning to Claire and Ellie, said, "And from what I've seen of you two, you're getting on really well with the other girls, so"—she twisted behind her and picked up her laptop—"here's how I think we should do this," she said to her now captivated audience. "Bea and Perry, I want you to talk to Henry Greenhill and see if he's got anything to say. You know, like did he notice Mercy during the evening? Was she up to anything? Also, see if you can find out his whereabouts from about nine until say midnight. Did he see anyone or anything out of place? That sort of stuff."

Bea tipped her head at Perry, and he grinned. "We can do that."

"Then also see if you can talk to the barman Jarvis Freeth. Find out what Mercy was drinking. Who she talked to. If she left the bar. Did he notice anything unusual? Oh, and see if you can find out his movements between the same time period as well."

Bea's stomach fluttered. This was much more exciting than sitting in on interviews as she'd done back at Drew Castle. *We're going to get to talk to people ourselves.*

Em turned to Ellie and Claire. "Can you two go to the spa and see what you can glean from the birthday girls? Try and find out what they did last night after we left. Also, what do they know of Mercy? Did she have any allergies?" She addressed them all. "We're really looking to see if anyone noticed anything out of the ordinary or has any information that could help us piece together what happened. I'm also interested in anything that can paint a picture of our victim. Does that make sense?"

Bea nodded along with the others. *Hold on did she say victim?* "So you think it's murder, do you?" she asked.

Em shrugged. "We don't know for sure. As I said earlier, the doctor thinks it was something she ate or drank that killed her. Whether that was an accident or not, they haven't been able to determine yet. So until the autopsy report comes back and says otherwise, we have to treat it as a suspicious death right now."

"And how will we get a copy of the report once it's available?" Perry asked, his brow creased.

An enormous grin spread across Em's face. "Don't you worry about that. I have a plan. In the meantime, while you're all off sleuthing, I'm going to do background checks on all the staff and guests." She winked. "I still have access to the PaIRS system. I suggest we reconvene here around one for lunch."

"Got it," Perry said as he stood. He turned to Bea. "Come on, Miss Marple. Let's do our thing," he said, trying unsuccessfully to stifle a grin as he held out a hand to her.

She grabbed it at the same time as rolling her eyes. "We'll see you all later."

Claire rose too. "Come on, El. We'd best get our robes, then go down to the spa. It's a tough job, but someone has to do it," she said, laughing as Ellie leaped up to join her.

Em smiled, then her face cleared. "Just stay together, all right?"

Bea paused at the door as her heart jumped. Stay together? *Yikes! Is she really concerned there's a killer on the loose?*

12

11:15 AM, SATURDAY 13 MARCH

Making their way down the stairs at Chasingham House, Bea and Perry turned left at the bottom and headed towards the bar. They had agreed they would start with Jarvis Freeth, the bartender, and hoped they might stumble across Greenhill while he was doing his rounds later.

As they entered the bar, there was no Jarvis to be seen, but Bea spied Vikki sitting on a small leather sofa in the corner, a cup of coffee on the low table in front of her. She spotted Bea and waved. "We may as well talk to her while we're here," Bea muttered as she led Perry over towards the literary agent sitting on her own.

"Hey, Vikki. How are you holding up?" Bea asked, stopping just in front of the table.

Vikki shrugged, her thin shoulders jutting around her ears. "It's the first time I've seen a dead body," she said, her voice trembling.

"Oh, Vikki, I'm so sorry," Bea said, sitting down next to her on the sofa and taking her hand. "It must have been a dreadful shock for you."

Vikki slowly ducked her head in agreement. "That's why

I couldn't face going to the spa with the others. I needed a coffee and some time to just be, you know."

Bea dropped her hand. "I'm sorry. Would you like us to leave you—"

"No, no." Vikki shook her head violently and grabbed Bea's arm. "Please. Stay. I don't really like being on my own."

Bea smiled and nodded to Perry, who took the armchair next to them. Vikki let go of Bea's hand and, leaning back, crossed her legs, her large white trainers dangling off her spindly legs. Bea looked deep into Vikki's brown eyes, searching for any telltale signs of guilt or discomfort, but Vikki folded her hands primly in her lap, looking comfortable and relaxed. Vikki's gaze flitted between Bea and Perry. It seemed clear she wanted to talk but didn't know where to start.

Bea took a deep breath. "I'm so sorry for your loss, Vikki. I know Mercy was your friend."

Vikki hesitated, then let out a deep sigh. "I wouldn't say she is…I mean…was really a friend. She was the daughter of friends of my parents. My mother felt sorry for her not knowing anyone in London, so I took her out with me a few times, but, you know, she wasn't really part of our close-knit group. We tried to make her feel welcome, of course." She picked up her cup and took a sip of coffee. "Then my mother asked me to invite her along this weekend, and Cammy was fine with it, so I did."

"Did Mercy work in London?" Perry asked.

"Yes, she worked at a fashion house in the city, although I'm not sure what her role was exactly. I think she may have been a buyer of some sort."

"She was American, wasn't she? How did she end up in London?"

"Her parents moved here when her father was posted to the American embassy. Mercy got married when she was in her early twenties, but something went wrong. Anyway, when her parents moved over here, they brought her with them." Vikki paused, looking down at her hands. "He died, I think."

"Who did?" Bea asked gently.

"Mercy's husband. That's all I really know."

Poor Mercy, to lose her husband so young. Bea could imagine how hard that must have been for her. *At least I had Sam to help me through when James died. Maybe that's why...* "Mercy was drinking quite heavily last night. Was that usual?"

Vikki smiled wryly. "Yes, she was." Then she frowned. "Now you mention it, when she's been out with us, she's always drunk more than anyone else. I'd not really noticed it before. Do you think she had a drinking problem?"

"It's possible, I suppose," Bea replied. *Could excessive drinking have led to her death in any way?*

"When we left the bar, you were all still here," Perry said. "Did you stay much longer?"

"No. Mel helped me take Mercy up to her room at about ten-thirty," Vikki said, her eyes narrowing as a scowl appeared on her face. "As you pointed out, she'd had way too much to drink and was not in a fit state." She swallowed, and her face cleared. "She protested at first and said she didn't want to miss out, but once we got her into the lift, she stopped resisting."

It was clear from her manner, she wasn't happy about having had to babysit Mercy.

"Where in the room did you leave her?" Bea asked, watching Vikki closely.

"By the window," Vikki replied, her voice wavering slightly. "We sat her down in a chair by the table there. She

63

seemed to have sobered up a bit by then, so we said good-night and left her there." Vikki looked down at the table, her eyes fixated on her empty coffee cup.

Hadn't Em said there had been an empty glass found in Mercy's room? "Did she have a drink with her when you took her up?"

"Yes." Vikki looked up. "She still had what remained of her cocktail in her hand."

"Did you go straight to bed after that?" Perry asked.

"Not straight away, no. Mel and I went back downstairs and joined the others, but we didn't stay much longer. It all fell flat, you know. Anyway, just before eleven, Mel said she had an online webinar to attend, so we all called it a night. I went up to my room."

"And did you leave your room at all after that?"

Bea glanced at Perry. He wasn't even pretending to be subtle about it now.

Vikki shook her head. "No, of course not."

Bea raised an eyebrow. There was something about how quickly Vikki had spoken and the way her eyes now darted around the room that made her suspect she wasn't being entirely truthful. *But why would Vikki lie?*

Vikki wiggled her fingers, her hands still together in her lap. She shook her head sadly. "I should have stayed with her, shouldn't I?"

"No, Vikki. You had no reason to believe she was in any danger, did you?"

Vikki frowned. "No, of course not."

Bea laid a hand on her arm. "Then you have no reason to blame yourself."

The woman was struggling to maintain her composure. *Poor Vikki.* She might not have been close to Mercy, but it was clear she still carried a sense of responsibility for her.

Vikki gave her a weak smile. "Thank you." Then she grimaced. "I hope my mother feels the same way when she finds out."

"Did you like Mercy, Vikki?"

Bea stifled a gasp as she removed her hand from Vikki's arm. Perry's question had seemed to come out of nowhere.

Vikki hesitated, her eyes flicking away from Perry's scrutiny as she stared at a point somewhere beyond his shoulder. Her fingers fidgeted with the clasp on her jumpsuit. When she spoke, her voice was measured. "I didn't dislike her. I barely knew her, really. My mother insisted I included her with my friends, so I suppose I resented her a bit for that. She wasn't one of us, you know."

Bea observed Vikki closely, taking note of the slight quiver in her voice and the way her eyes refused to meet Perry's. *What's she hiding? Was she getting fed up of looking out for someone who "wasn't one of us"? So fed up she would—*

"Did Mercy have any allergies that you know of?" Perry wasn't letting up.

Vikki shrugged. "Nothing that I'm aware of."

"Any medication? Was she on drugs?"

Vikki shook her head. "Again, not that I know of." She shifted in her seat and crossed her arms. "You're asking a lot of questions, Perry."

She has a point...

"I'm so sorry," Perry said, sounding sheepish. "I'm dreadfully curious about things. My bad." He gave her a charming smile.

Vikki stared at him for a moment, then she uncrossed her arms and smiled back. "No, I'm sorry. I didn't mean to snap." She ran her fingers through her highlighted brown hair. "It's just been a horrid day so far. What with finding Mercy, then that policeman, you know, the little one with the enormous nose, asking me lots of questions." She let out a deep sigh. "I'm just tired."

"Why don't you go to your room and lie down for a bit? You might feel better," Perry suggested kindly.

"I think you might be right," Vikki said, rising from the sofa. "I'll see you later."

"What do you think of that?" Perry whispered when Vikki was out of earshot.

"Well, I think your questioning technique could do with a little improvement."

"Not me, silly," he said, giving a frustrated sigh. "I mean her. Don't you think she's hiding something?"

So Perry didn't think Vikki was being completely honest with them either... Bea shrugged her shoulders. "Everyone has secrets, Perry," she said, offering a wan smile. "You must know that after all the investigations we've been involved in over the last year. The question is: does the secret have anything to do with Mercy's death?"

13

11:40 AM, SATURDAY 13 MARCH

Bea sat on the sofa in the empty bar, her fingers drumming lightly on the low mahogany table in front of her. The sun filtered through the large windows on the other side of the room, casting warm rays on the tasteful floral wallpaper adorned with watercolour paintings of quaint English land-scapes on the wall over by the bar. *There's an unmistakable elegance that permeates Chasingham House,* she thought.

"Where is everyone?" Perry asked.

She looked around again. Jarvis was still absent, and she hadn't seen a server pass by for ages either. *I could really do with a coffee right now.*

As if sensing her need, Greenhill, the tall upright manager of the hotel and spa, walked in and approached them. "Lady Rossex, Mr Juke, is everything alright? Can I get you anything?" He stopped before them, and Bea caught a whiff of his cologne, a blend of woodsy and citrus notes that seemed to suit the man's polished demeanour.

"Actually, Mr. Greenhill," Bea said, smiling. "We wouldn't say no to a large pot of coffee."

"And maybe a few biscuits?" Perry added.

"Of course, my lady and sir," Greenhill replied, his voice smooth and controlled. "Let me get that organised for you." He moved to turn away.

Hold on. This could be a good time to ask him a few questions.

As if reading her mind, Perry shot her a look, then said, "I hope today hasn't been too trying for you, Mr Greenhill?"

The man halted, then turned to face them again. His dark eyes flicked to Perry, concern sparking behind his well-trimmed beard. "I hope you don't feel as if we've been neglecting our guests, Mr Juke. Of course, with the police here asking questions and their crime scene officers running around upstairs, it has been a bit difficult to—"

Perry raised his hand and shook his head. "No, not at all, Mr Greenhill. That wasn't what I meant. Everything has been perfect, as always. I was more concerned you and the staff must be finding the death of a guest difficult, you know, emotionally."

"Thank you for your concern, Mr Juke," Greenhill said, giving Perry a polite smile that didn't quite reach his eyes. "But we're fine."

Bea stifled a frustrated sigh. *I think he's going to be difficult to get anything out of.*

However, Perry seemed to be unfazed by the slight disconnect. "And especially for you being the person who found her dead body."

Greenhill nodded, then said, "I'll go and get your drinks." He hurried out of the room as if he was being chased by demons.

"Oh dear," Perry said, pulling a face as he watched the man flee. "I thought he'd be more forthcoming than that."

"Think about it, Perry. His job is to be discreet. He's not

going to go blabbing to us about Mercy's death. We need to think of another way to get him to talk."

"Well," Perry said, rising. "I'm going to leave that to you. I've just spotted Jarvis at the bar, so I'm going to grill him."

Bea smiled. "Try to be subtle."

"Subtle is my middle name," Perry said as he glided away.

———

"Your coffee, my lady." Greenhill was back and seemed relieved to see Perry over at the bar talking to Jarvis. He placed a large coffee pot in the middle of the table, then unloaded cups, saucers, a milk jug, a bowl of sugar, and a plate of cookies and mini pastries. He spread them around the pot. "Is there anything else, Lady Rossex?"

Yes, I need to ask you about last night! An idea struck her.

"Actually, Mr Greenhill, there is something."

He raised an eyebrow.

"I didn't want to bother you earlier. I know it's been a… er…busy day for you so far. But last night I lost a scarf. A Hermes one. It's black with white roses on it and belongs to my mother. I had it wrapped around my hair initially, but later I let my hair down, and now I can't remember what I did with it. I wonder if you've seen it lying around anywhere?"

She swallowed and gave him a sweet smile. Well, it wasn't completely a lie. She *had* been wearing a scarf, and she *had* taken it out of her hair halfway through the evening. But she'd tied it around her wrist and must have put it down in Perry's suite. But Mr Greenhill didn't need to know that.

"I don't believe I have, my lady. And as far as I know, nothing has been handed in." He frowned, then continued, "I do remember your ladyship wearing the article last night, and

I'm certain when I came into the bar to check on Jarvis after you all left, it wasn't here."

"Maybe I dropped it between the bar and my room?" she suggested, her eyes wide. *Come on. Give me something...*

Henry adjusted his cufflinks and slowly shook his head. "I did a walkabout of the premises before calling it a night, as I do every evening. I didn't see it, I'm afraid."

"And what time do you do your walkabout?"

"It all depends on what time the guests finish. Last night it was relatively early, so I started about eleven."

"And what does your walkabout involve?"

"I check the restaurant to make sure it's all ready for breakfast. Then I go to the bar and check on Jarvis to make sure he's not had any issues. Then I do a quick visit to each floor just to make sure—" He hesitated and gave a wry smile. "No one is lost or unable to get into their room—"

Bea stifled a giggle. *He means he makes sure no one has collapsed drunk in a corridor or is having a noisy party in their room.*

"And then I return downstairs and make sure the night porter has everything he needs before I go to my apartment, which is on-site."

"So when you did your walkabout last night, you didn't notice my scarf on the floor anywhere?" Bea asked, hoping she wasn't pushing too hard.

But Greenhill now seemed to be in a more forthcoming mood. "Sorry, my lady, but no."

"Maybe someone picked it up?"

"I didn't see them pick anything up," Greenhill said, his brow furrowing slightly.

See who? Bea's heart sped up. Greenhill had seen someone last night. She leaned forward slightly, her curiosity piqued.

"When did you see someone, Mr Greenhill?"

"Around eleven-fifteen. I was going up the staff staircase. I saw someone descending the main stairs between the third and second floor at the other end of the corridor."

"Did you recognise them?" she asked, then added quickly, "Maybe I can ask them if they saw my scarf?"

Greenhill shook his head. "No. Sorry. They were dressed entirely in black," he recalled, his gaze fixed on a point somewhere above her head as he seemed to dredge up the memory. "It was difficult to make out many details in the dim light, but she seemed to move quickly, as though in a hurry."

So it had been a woman. Bea's mind raced at this new piece of information. Could this shadowy figure have had something to do with Mercy's death?

"And you can't be any more specific, Mr Greenhill?"

"Um, well…" The manager paused, appearing to gather his thoughts. "She had a certain gracefulness to her movements despite being in a hurry. And she was at least five foot ten, I'd say." He shifted his weight, his Adam's apple bobbing as he swallowed. "Sorry. As I said, I don't know who it was." He shrugged apologetically, spreading his hands wide.

"Of course," she conceded, though she noticed the slight narrowing of his eyes. *Maybe the hotel manager is just being discreet.*

"Did you see anyone else while you were on your walk-about, Mr Greenhill?"

He straightened up. "No, my lady. But I will enquire at the front desk to make sure no one has found your scarf and handed it to them for safekeeping."

Bea smiled. "Indeed. Thank you for your help, Mr Greenhill."

Bea's mind whirled with questions and possibilities. "Well, that was interesting," she muttered to herself. A tall woman in black moving quickly around just after the time of Mercy's death. Was it somehow connected? Her heart raced. Could it have been the killer? Greenhill had said the woman was tall. *It's most likely Mel, Cammy, or Flick then.* Vikki was a good few inches shorter than the others.

"Well, I have something," Perry said smugly, making her start. He lowered himself onto the sofa next to her and grabbed the coffeepot.

"Me too," Bea replied, holding out her cup.

"You first then," he said, taking the milk and adding it to his coffee.

Bea told him about the mysterious woman Henry Greenhill had seen around the time of Mercy's death.

"Nice work," Perry said when she'd finished. "So…a tall woman. It must have been Flick, Cammy, or Mel then."

"That's what I was thinking. But before we get too carried away, it might *not* have anything to do with Mercy, so we need to keep an open mind."

He gave a sharp nod. "Agreed. We'll tell Em and see how she wants to follow it up."

Bea smiled. "So…what did Jarvis tell you?"

Perry glanced over at the lanky-framed man polishing the wooden bar top and leaned towards her. "Well, he was on the bar all evening. He has to stay until the last guest leaves, which last night was about ten to eleven. He then cleaned up and did some restocking behind the bar until about eleven thirty."

"Did he see anyone during that time?"

"He said Greenhill was around doing his late night checks. He came into the bar around eleven, and they chatted for five minutes or so, then he left to do his walkabout. He returned at around twenty-five past eleven as Jarvis was just finishing up, and they said goodnight."

Bea nodded. Jarvis had confirmed the timings Greenhill had given her.

"I asked him if he noticed any unusual behaviour from anyone yesterday, and in particular Mercy Bright. He said it was quieter than usual with only the two groups here, but everyone seemed friendly and looked like they were having a good time. He said Mercy was drinking champagne at lunchtime here in the bar, then moved onto cocktails in the evening. She was drinking the strawberry sensation, which he made himself. It's a mix of crushed strawberries, vodka, rum, strawberry syrup, and lemonade."

Bea's forehead creased. "I don't think I tried that one; did you?"

Perry shook his head. "I'm not a great fan of fruit in drinks. Anyway, I asked him if he noticed if anyone left the bar that evening. He said most of us left at some point or another — you know, to use the toilets and such, but..." Perry paused for effect.

Bea rolled her eyes. "But what?"

"But...he thinks Mercy disappeared around nine and was gone for about thirty minutes."

Interesting... She remembered Mercy coming back into the bar but hadn't realised she'd been gone that long. "Did he notice anyone else absent at the same time?"

Perry shook his head. "Unfortunately, no. He said we, as in our party, placed an order for a round of cocktails just as she left, so he was busy with that."

Bea sighed. *That's disappointing.* She'd hoped maybe Mercy had had an argument with someone and that person was her killer. *Stop! We still don't know she was killed. Maybe there's a simpler explanation. Strawberries...* "Could she have had an allergic reaction to strawberries, do you think?"

Perry tilted his head to one side, pulling a face as he held up his screen. "Great minds! I was just looking up strawberry allergies. Turns out some fruits can be as deadly as peanuts when it comes to allergies." Grabbing a cookie, he rose. "Should we head back to my room and catch up with the others?"

"Absolutely," Bea replied, pushing herself up from the sofa. She was keen to hear what Em thought of the mysterious woman in black. And, more importantly, would Em know yet if Mercy's death had been an accident or not? Had it been a tragic reaction to some seemingly harmless ingredient? Or something more sinister?

14

LUNCHTIME, SATURDAY 13 MARCH

The sun streamed through the huge glass windows of Perry's suite, casting a ray of white across the plush carpet. Bea adjusted her position on the floral-patterned window seat and closed her eyes, enjoying the warmth on her face. The vibrant atmosphere of the room seemed to lift her spirits after a long morning of investigation.

"So while we've been hard at it, you've been lounging around enjoying the view," Ellie said as she swept into the room and bounded towards her. She was followed closely by Claire wrapped up in a white towelling robe, looking almost too casual for the carefully curated elegance of Chasingham House.

"Yes. Bea and I decided in the end it was too lovely to be investigating a death. We've actually been sitting in the sun most of the morning," Perry replied with a grin from a chair in front of the fireplace.

"Ha!" Ellie replied as she settled onto the sofa opposite Perry while Claire sat next to Em on a large navy-blue sofa in front of a low coffee table. Em was flicking through crime scene photos on her laptop.

There was a knock on the door, and François, the server, entered the room, approaching the group with a professional smile. "Your lunch is almost ready. Would you like us to set it up for you at the dining table over there?" He indicated the large polished mahogany table on the other side of the room.

"Absolutely," Ellie said, and everyone nodded their agreement. "That sounds wonderful."

Bea looked at Em. Would she make them all wait until after they'd eaten before they shared what they'd learned? Had the others found out anything useful? She glanced at Perry sitting in a blue-and-green tartan armchair. He was fidgeting with excitement.

Bea suppressed a sigh of relief when Em said, "Ellie and Claire, do you want to start?"

"Only Cammy, Mel, and Flick were in the spa, and they were a bit subdued," Claire said, looking at Ellie.

"Flick appeared rather nervous," Ellie shared, leaning in conspiratorially. "She hardly said a word to the others. Like she had a secret."

"What about Mel and Cammy? Were they acting strange as well?" Bea asked.

"Ah, Mel." Claire sighed, shaking her head. "She was a picture of cool composure on the surface—" She paused for effect. "But there was a definite tension lurking beneath. I could practically feel it radiating off her."

"And Cammy was just babbling away to everyone as if she thought if she kept talking, she could ignore what had happened," Ellie added.

Bea furrowed her brow. The feeling of unease settled in her bones and grew heavier when she recalled talking to Vikki. Were all the birthday girls hiding something?

"Perhaps they're just on edge because of their friend's

death," Em suggested. "In my experience, people react differently when someone dies unexpectedly."

"Cammy was saying how drunk everyone had been last night, especially Mercy. She suggested that maybe she'd died from alcohol poisoning." She held up her hand. "I'll be honest, I didn't even know that was a thing, dying from one evening I mean. Then she wondered if maybe Mercy had taken drugs, but Flick said she wasn't into that."

That fits with what Vikki said.

"Apart from that, there isn't really much to tell you. Mel and Vikki took Mercy up to her room at about ten-thirty and left her there, then came back to the bar to rejoin the others. Then, at about ten to eleven, they all went to bed. Mel said she had an online thing."

She looked over at Ellie, who said, "Yeah, she told me she had an online webinar that started at eleven." She shrugged. "None of them claim to have left their rooms after retiring for the night."

Perry gasped. "But Henry Greenhill saw a woman dressed in black going down the stairs between the third and second floor at about eleven-fifteen," he blurted out.

There was a start from Ellie, and Claire raised her hand to her chest.

Em raised an eyebrow. "Well, that's interesting."

Bea's heart skipped a beat. *So one of them is lying! But which one?*

"Who did he think it was?" Em asked Perry.

Bea jumped in. "He didn't recognise them. He just said he was fairly sure it was a woman, and she was tall, at least five-ten."

"So it would be Cammy, Flick, or Mel!" Perry cried with a flourish. "Vikki is too short to—"

Em put up her hand. "Okay. Okay. Before we get too

carried away, let's just stick to what we know — Henry Greenhill saw someone." She paused, running her fingers through her bouncy tight black curls. "But until we know more about Mercy's death and if it was accidental or not, I suggest we park it under 'things to follow up', okay?"

They nodded just as the door opened. The scent of warm bread and fresh coffee wafted into the room as the server wheeled in a cart laden with an enticing array of sandwiches, quiches, and assorted finger foods. Bea's stomach rumbled loudly, a reminder she'd not eaten yet today.

"Food!" Perry declared, his eyes lighting up as he surveyed the spread before them. "I don't know about you lot, but I'm famished."

"Me too," Ellie said. Her gaze lingered on a plate of delicate cucumber sandwiches, their crusts trimmed off just so.

"Come on," Perry said as he stood up, moving towards the table along the wall where the server was laying out the food. "We'll need our energy if we're going to get to the bottom of this mystery."

After they helped themselves to food and returned to their seats, Em turned to Bea and Perry. "So you spoke to Greenhill then?"

Bea gave them an account of what Greenhill had told her, then Perry detailed his chat with Jarvis, the bartender.

When they finished, Em cleared her throat. "Right, let me give you a summary of the key points we've gathered so far." She picked up her cup of tea and took a sip. "Okay. So Mercy was drinking heavily throughout the evening and may have left the bar for a period of about thirty minutes at some point." She scrolled through the notes on her phone. "Around ten-thirty, Mel and Vikki took her up to her room. They left her in her chair with a drink — likely one of those strawberry sensations made by Jarvis. Mel and Vikki returned to the bar afterwards," she continued, "but it wasn't long before everyone dispersed to their rooms. Mel claims she had an online webinar to attend, while Cammy, Vikki, and Flick all insisted they went straight to bed. Meanwhile," Em went on, her voice growing more animated, "Greenhill started his nightly walkabout at around five past eleven. At approximately quarter past eleven, he saw a tall woman dressed in black descending the stairs between the third and second floor. He returned to the bar ten minutes later and said goodnight to Jarvis. As far as we know, according to Vikki, Mercy had no food allergies, wasn't on any medication, and didn't do drugs." She looked at the others. "Have I missed anything?"

Bea shook her head and took a bite of a smoked salmon and cream cheese sandwich. It didn't feel like they had that much.

Perry put up his hand. "When will we get Mercy's medical records or get hold of her family to confirm she had no allergies? It's just that she had a lot of strawberries and—"

"But if she had an issue with strawberries, then surely she wouldn't have been drinking cocktails with strawberries in?" Claire said, frowning.

"I know. That's my point. If she *didn't* know she had an allergy to them, then maybe that's what killed her?"

"It's possible, but so far I've been unable to get hold of Mercy's medical records. I have, however, been doing some background work." She tapped the screen of her mobile phone.

Bea leaned forward, eager to hear what Em had found out about their victim.

"Mercy Bright, real name Mercedes, was thirty-six and born in upstate New York. Her father is an American diplomat and her mother is a novelist. She went to the

Fashion Institute of Technology in the city, where she did a degree in Fashion Design. She went to work at the New York office of Marie Claire. Married at twenty-five. Husband was Ross Cole, a lawyer and Harvard graduate, son of the New York district attorney. He died two months after they were married. They fished him out of the East River. His death was recorded as suicide. Not long after, Mercy moved with her parents to Washington DC and then six months ago here to London. She was a freelance fashion buyer. She lived with her parents in a flat in London provided by the American embassy. Financially, she's pretty solid. She has no police record." She dropped her phone back onto the table and looked around the room. "Any questions?"

"What do we do now?" Perry piped up.

"We finish lunch. Then we go back out there and see what else we can find. I'm going to try to steal DS Meed away for five minutes and see what he can tell me. My gut's telling me he's not a big fan of Rivers, so he might be willing to help me. I suggest you head back to the spa and join the girls. Now the shock has warn off, they might be more communicative. And if not—" She smiled. "You may as well enjoy the rest of the afternoon."

Perry huffed. "Is there really nothing else we can do?"

Em sighed. "I know it's frustrating, and there's still much we don't know at this stage. All we can do is keep our eyes and ears open and be patient until the autopsy report comes in."

Bea looked over at Perry, who was on the edge of his seat, the heels of his beautiful designer shoes tapping up and down on the rug. *That's easier said than done!*

15

1:45 PM, SATURDAY 13 MARCH

Bea closed the door of her bedroom at Chasingham House and shuffled in her spa slippers along the panelled corridor of the first floor. She turned right at the end and descended the main staircase. Tightening the heavy white towelling robe around her, she wasn't sure she was in the mood for the spa this afternoon. But then, as Em had pointed out, there wasn't much more they could do at the moment. She smiled. At least she'd had time to catch up with her son Sam again. They'd finished lessons for the day at his boarding school, and they dedicated Saturday afternoons at Wilton College to sport. He'd told her in an excited voice that he was trying tennis for the first time. She smiled. Sam was more used to team sports, and like his father, had been making a name for himself by playing cricket and rugby for the school. It would be interesting to see how motivated he would be when playing purely for himself. As she reached the bottom step, a small grey-haired woman came hurtling past her and stopped at the reception desk.

"Where's Mr Greenhill?" she cried, flapping her hands

just above the low wooded counter. "I must speak to him urgently."

Bea slowed down. Instead of heading left to the spa, she turned right and stealthily made her way towards two leather armchairs with their backs to reception. She quietly dropped herself into one and listened.

"Mrs Everett, what on earth is the matter?" Henry Greenhill's voice was calm and low.

"Oh, Mr Greenhill, something awful has happened," the women said in a shaky voice. "I have to tell someone because I don't want to get blamed and—"

"Mrs Everett!" Chasingham House's usually unflappable manager hissed, "Please calm down."

There was movement behind Bea. *Oh no! Pleased don't move away from here...*

"Now tell me what's happened."

Bea breathed a sigh of relief. Greenhill had moved himself and Mrs Everett away from the reception desk and towards where she was sitting, presumably thinking the area was empty. Bea slunk further down in her chair.

"Mr Parks' potassium chloride has gone missing from his suite. It's dangerous in its undiluted form, you know, and I'm really worried I'm going to be—"

"When did you realise it was gone?" Greenhill asked urgently.

"Just now. I went up to check on his rooms. I'm off tomorrow, and I wanted it all to be ready for him when he gets back on Monday morning. Anyway, I noticed a smudge on the door of the bathroom cabinet. I opened the door so I could hold it while I wiped it clean, and that's when I noticed it was gone—"

"It being the entire bottle of potassium chloride?"

Bea slowly took her phone out of her robe pocket and typed 'potassium chloride' into her browser.

"It's a large white plastic container. He buys it in bulk because he has to take it each day for his hypokalaemia."

Potassium chloride, also known as potassium salt, is used as a medication to treat and prevent low blood potassium. The concentrated version should be diluted before use. Potassium chloride is used in lethal injections... Bea stifled a cry. *Oh my goodness!* Could the missing potassium chloride have been used to kill Mercy?

"Isn't it possible he could have taken it away with him on his trip?" Greenhill asked calmly.

"No. He doesn't travel with it. He has similar supplies at all of his homes and a much smaller bottle, already diluted, for when he's away. And anyway, I saw it there when I tidied up the day he left. He'd left it out on the side of the basin. I was the one who put it back in the cabinet."

Bea needed to tell Em — now. Except she couldn't move, or Greenhill and the woman would see her. She took a slow quiet breath in. And out...

"Who has keys to Mr Parks' apartment apart from you and me?"

"Only Mr Parks," she replied, her voice now lower and calmer.

Bea frowned. *But what about his daughter? Does Mel Parks have a key as well?*

"And where do you keep your key, Mrs Everett? Is it possible someone borrowed it?"

The housekeeper sounded indignant. "I keep it on my person with all my other keys when I'm here working, and when I'm not, it's locked in the safe in my office."

"And I locked mine in my office," Greenhill said thoughtfully. "Well, thank you for bringing this to my attention. I'll do my best to get to the bottom of what's happened to it."

The woman huffed. "Well, I hope so. He's back on Monday and won't be best pleased that it's missing."

Bea listened as their footsteps hurried away. *Is it safe to move now?* She slowly turned and peeped around the side of her chair. The coast was clear. She jumped up, and pulling her belt tight, she scurried up the stairs as fast as her hotel slippers would allow.

16

2:15 PM, SATURDAY 13 MARCH

"I wonder who else was aware of Mr Parks' medical condition," Bea said as she took a sip from a glass of water in Perry's suite.

"Lots of people, I would imagine," Perry replied, waving his mobile phone in front of him. "According to this, he's been trying to raise awareness for the condition and has given lots of interviews about it over the last few years. This is a series about rare diseases in the *Sunday Times* a few weeks ago, and he featured in it."

Bea twirled the rings on her right hand. The person who had stolen it would not only have needed to know of Mr Parks' medical condition but also that he kept a supply at his rooms here *and* had been able to gain access to it. *That should narrow it down...*

"What about Greenhill?" Perry said, lowering his voice as he looked over at Em, who was on her mobile over by the window.

The Chasingham House manager not only had a key to the suite, so he could have taken the potassium chloride, but he also had the opportunity to poison Mercy in her room when he had supposedly been doing his walkabout. "It could be. But why would he want to kill a guest?" she whispered back.

Em cut the call and placed her mobile phone on the table. She turned to Bea with a mix of determination and weariness in her eyes. "I pulled in a favour, and that was the pathologist's assistant. The autopsy is scheduled for later this afternoon, so the police should have some results later today."

Bea nodded, feeling a knot of anticipation tightening in her chest. She knew the upcoming autopsy report would be a crucial piece of the puzzle. "It's hard not knowing if Mercy's death was an accident or murder, isn't it?"

Em sighed as she moved over to join Bea by the window. "Exactly. I can't put pressure on Rivers to let me in on what's going on; if it turns out Mercy's death was an accident, then none of it will be relevant." She dropped onto the window seat beside Bea and crossed her arms.

The atmosphere in the room had shifted, weighed down by the newfound knowledge of the missing potassium chloride. Bea glanced over at Perry, noting his furrowed brow and uneasy expression that seemed to mirror her own concerns.

"Mercy was drinking heavily last night," he said. "Could someone have spiked her drink?"

"We certainly can't rule it out," Em said, rising from the window seat and moving to the table to pick up her phone. "I'm going to see if Rivers knows about it yet. He'll need to tell the pathologist so they can test to see if Mercy was poisoned by potassium chloride." She quickly typed a message and pressed send.

"Can't the police arrange a search of the guest's rooms?" Perry asked. "Then if anyone has the potassium chloride, we'll know they're up to no good."

"Until they know it was potassium chloride that killed her, they won't be able to get a warrant."

Bea frowned. "Can't the police just ask the guests if they can search their rooms?"

Em gave a wry smile. "They could, but if a guest refuses to co-operate, then there will be nothing Rivers can do to make them. The risk is that by asking, he might tip someone off that they're looking for something, and that will give them time to dispose of it."

Bea mentally slapped her forehead. *Of course!* That could ruin everything. She still had so much to learn about the subtly of policing. In the past, Simon, Perry's future husband and an ex-Fenshire detective, had tried to instil in her and Perry how important it was not to interfere with police procedures, encouraging them to share everything they found with Fitzwilliam immediately so he could do things properly and the culprit could be convicted once caught. But the truth had been that they'd mostly run around willy-nilly, asking questions and stumbling upon clues, merely paying lip service to Simon's warnings. It had been a miracle they hadn't jeopardised any of the cases with their unconventional approach. Maybe it was a tribute to Fitzwilliam's professionalism that he'd been able to make and support a case despite their bumblings. But since the murder investigation at Drew Castle at the beginning of this year when, through necessity, Fitzwilliam had asked her, Perry, and Simon to assist him, she'd gained a newfound respect for him and his colleagues.

What would Fitzwilliam make of this case? she wondered. *How would he react to Rivers refusing to let PaIRS be involved?* She smiled to herself, imagining him towering over the balding head of the Chase DCI. Would he, like Em, decide to investigate Mercy's murder in spite of River's attitude? *Oh, yes!* He was like a dog with a bone once an investigation started, and Rivers wasn't strong enough to wrestle it away from him. It was one of the things she admired about him. His tenacity in seeking the truth. Without it, she would never have found out what had really happened to her late husband fifteen years ago. *And, of course, there's also his rugged good looks*, a voice said inside her head. *Stop it, Bea!* She needed to get a grip and focus on the job in hand. That was definitely something Fitzwilliam *would* do.

17

2:45 PM, SATURDAY 13 MARCH

Bea hugged her knees, her gaze wandering to the vibrant flowers that swayed gently in the breeze outside as she sat on the window seat in Perry's suite in Chasingham House. The sunlight filtering through the glass panes cast a warm glow over the room, contradicting the sombre atmosphere that hung heavily in the air. Bea released her arms and rubbed her temples, feeling a headache bubbling up inside. If only they knew if this was a murder investigation or not. She looked over to where Em was typing on her laptop. *If I'm fed up with this, I can't imagine how she must be feeling.*

There was a knock on the door. Perry sprang up. "That must be coffee," he said, heading towards the door. "Come in," he shouted. The door opened and a lanky man with short dark hair walked hesitantly into the room.

"DS Meed," Em rose, smiling. "Thank you for coming. I hope it wasn't a...er...problem?"

Meed returned her smile. "Rivers has gone back to the station. He's waiting for the autopsy report."

"Great," Em said as she gestured for him to sit by her.

"We've just been mulling over the potassium chloride conundrum. What's Rivers take on it?"

Meed sat down and crossed one long leg over the other. "He's informed the pathologist just in case it's pertinent to the case, but he's still of the view Mercy's death was an accident and therefore it's not relevant."

Really? Is he right? Maybe someone, possibly Greenhill, had stolen the potassium chloride, but it wasn't connected to Mercy's death? Maybe it was just a red herring. Perhaps they had stolen it with the intention of selling it on? But who would want to buy it? And what were the odds something so potentially dangerous would go missing at the same time as Mercy had been found dead? Bea smiled wryly. Fitzwilliam's voice echoed in her head, telling her he didn't trust coincidences. Right now, Bea had to agree with him.

"He thinks it's an accident based on what?" Em asked.

"We haven't been able to find anything that suggests anyone wanted her dead."

Em inclined her head slowly. "Yes, I would agree with that at the moment."

"Did Greenhill tell you about the mysterious woman in black?" Perry asked, his eyes dancing.

Meed nodded. "But he doesn't seem to know who it was."

"Did any of the others tell you they'd left their room last night after they all went up?" Em asked.

"No. They were all in their rooms according to their statements."

So they've told the police the same as they've told us? But if the manager had seen someone, then—

"One of them must be lying," Perry told him, a look of satisfaction on his face.

"It will probably turn out to be irrelevant," Meed said.

Perry pouted and looked away.

"Did anyone ring Mr Parks about the missing potassium chloride?" Em asked.

Meed gave a curt nod. "Yes. I did. Mr Parks made it very clear to me he didn't want to take this any further. He's in the States at the moment, so he's only just heard about Mercy's death. He's worried that having more police crawling all over the place, his words not mine, will give Chasingham House a bad reputation. He said he's sure there's a perfectly reasonable explanation for the medication going missing." He shrugged.

"But there might be fingerprints," Perry said, "that can tell you who was in Parks' suite and took the stuff."

"Unless it turns out it was potassium chloride that killed Mercy Bright, it will be more than Rivers' job's worth to call Forensics in to go through Parks' place without his cooperation."

"What about Henry Greenhill?" Bea asked, returning to Perry's earlier idea. "Could it have been him?"

Meed tilted his head to one side, then the other. "When I spoke to him, he insisted he hadn't been in Mr Parks' rooms and no one could have got hold of his set of keys. I even checked the safe in his office. The key was still there. Of course he could be lying." He paused, then continued, "I did learn one interesting piece of information from Mr Parks; his daughter has a key to his suite. He remembers giving it to her about a year ago when the hotel was full and she and a friend wanted to stay."

Mel? Could Mel have stolen the potassium chloride? But why would she want to kill Mercy? She was the only one in the group who hadn't met her before this weekend.

Perry jumped up. "Shouldn't you be interviewing her about it?"

Em shook her head. "Only if we find out potassium chloride was involved in Mercy's death." She turned to Meed. "While I was examining the—"

There was a knock, and the door to the room creaked open. With a, "Sorry to disturb you," a young server inched into the room, pushing a trolly containing tea and coffee things. They sat in silence while he unloaded the tray onto the large table by the wall, then watched as he hurried out.

"You were saying?" Meed said to Em as they all rose and made their way to the table.

"I was looking at the crime scene photos I took, and I couldn't see much. Did the SOCO team find anything?"

Meed shrugged. "They found nothing of relevance in her handbag—no EpiPen or card indicating a deadly allergy."

Bea glanced at Perry and pulled a face. *Another dead end.*

"However," Meed continued, "they did find something curious on the floor—a small artificial jewel that could have come from a pair of earrings maybe, although Mercy's were all intact." He pulled a piece of paper from inside his jacket. He unfolded it and passed it to Em.

"It looks like one of those stick-on jewels people use on their faces at festivals." She slid the picture across the table to Bea.

Bea put down her coffee and, leaning forward, picked up the picture. The diamond-like object was small, the size of a pen tip. "Maybe it's the centrepiece of a nose stud?" Bea said, slightly squinting.

Perry leaned over her shoulder. "It looks like an individual crystal to me. Do any of our guests have nose piercings?"

Bea frowned, then shook her head, handing the piece of paper to Perry. "No, I'm sure they don't."

"Could it belong to a previous guest?" Perry suggested, his slim fingers tracing the edges of the photograph. "I mean, if the room wasn't cleaned thoroughly, it might have been left behind."

"It's possible," Meed conceded, "but it's still worth looking into." He paused for a moment before carrying on, "As for Mercy's phone, they're still trying to unlock it. No luck yet."

"What about her parents?" Em asked. "Did you get hold of them yet?"

Meed shook his head. "When our officers arrived at their flat, the housekeeper told them they'd flown back to the States for a function a few hours previously. We checked their flight. It's not due to land for a while yet."

Bea tapped her foot impatiently, the soft thud of her slipper against the carpet barely audible. *Can't we catch a break?*

"And the contents of the glass?" Em asked, her voice tinged with anticipation.

"Still waiting on the analysis," Meed admitted, his goatee twitching as he frowned. "We should know more later today."

"Is it me, or does it seem like every road we go down, we find a big fat 'road closed' sign?" Perry cried.

Indeed!

"Welcome to policing," Meed muttered as a knock came at the door.

"Do I smell coffee?" Ellie asked as she strolled into the room, followed by Claire. "We have some juicy—" They both stopped dead when they saw DS Meed.

"Don't worry," Em said, moving towards them carrying her cup of tea. "DS Meed is on our side."

The sergeant made a saluting gesture with his hand and smiled. "At your service, ladies."

Ellie and Claire chuckled as they moved towards the tea and coffee.

"So what did you find out?" Em asked. She turned to Meed. "Ellie and Claire have been hanging out in the spa, keeping their eyes and ears open."

Ellie gave a huge grin as she picked up the coffeepot and poured herself a large black coffee. "Kind of like spies. But cuter."

Claire gave her a playful elbow as she grabbed the teapot. "Cammy, Vikki, Flick, and Mel were all there. You were right, Em. They seemed more relaxed than they were this morning, although we did wonder if Vikki and Flick have had some sort of argument as they barely spoke to each other."

Bea frowned. Flick and Vikki had been close friends ever since they'd been at school together. *I wonder what's going on there?*

"Anyway," Claire continued, "the chat was mainly about their love lives…" She looked over at DS Meed and blushed.

Ellie grinned at her friend and took up the narrative. "Cammy has just broken up with a complete idiot, by all accounts. He's been cheating on her for ages. She was trying to convince the others he was really sorry, but they told her he was a loser. Mel threatened to disown her if she went back to him. Cammy was upset and looked a bit guilty, didn't she, Claire?"

Claire nodded. "Yes, she did. And a little later I found out why. Cammy admitted to me that she'd spent an hour when she'd got back to her room last night FaceTiming with this ex-boyfriend of hers. He told her that he'd made a big mistake and would never cheat on her again. She's seriously thinking of giving him another chance."

So Cammy has an—

"So she couldn't have killed Mercy if she was online with her boyfriend at the time!" Perry cried.

Exactly!

Claire frowned. "Oh, yes. I hadn't thought of that. But hold on, you can't say anything to the police. She told me in strict confidence. She said the others would be furious if they found out. She'd promised them not to have any contact with him this weekend. She was on a bad boyfriend detox."

"Er, Claire," Ellie said, tipping her head in the direction of DS Meed, who was standing by the fireplace looking rather sheepish.

"Oh, rats! You can't tell anyone, sergeant. You have to promise." Claire looked at him with pleading eyes.

Meed cleared his throat. "Unless it turns into a murder investigation and we have to get proper alibis from people, then my lips are sealed. And even then, I'll not let anyone know you told me." He flashed her a smile, and she blushed.

"What about the others?" Perry asked, a dash of impatience in his voice.

Ellie walked back towards them with a cup of tea in her hand. "Mel is anti-men, or so she appears. Although, of course, that doesn't seem to stop her dating a bunch of famous and terribly gorgeous men...sorry... Anyway, later I was chatting with Cammy by the pool. She told me not to take any notice of Mel; she had her heart broken when she was in her mid-twenties and lived in New York, so now she's afraid of being hurt."

Bea stifled a yawn. *What does this have to do with anything? Where was the juicy stuff they promised? Hold on! Did Ellie say Mel lived in New York? Wasn't that where Mercy lived? They were about the same age, so that would be about ten years ago.* Was it just another coincidence?

"And then there's Flick," Claire said.

Bea was suddenly alert. "What about Flick?"

"Her marriage is on the rocks apparently."

Bea frowned. Was that what her cousin, Caroline, had

meant when she'd said Flick had been having trouble at home? "Did she tell you that?"

Claire shook her head. "Cammy told me. She said things had been difficult for them for a while. This weekend getaway was partly to give Flick space to decide if she's going to leave him or not."

Bea twisted the rings on her right hand. *Poor Flick. Poor Barney.* They'd got married only a few months after her and James.

"Is that it?" Perry said, sounding bored. "Is that the juicy gossip?"

"No, no." Ellie moved back to the table and put down her now empty cup. "Vikki was telling me she'd gone up to her room to sleep a bit before lunch, but she'd not been able to. So she left her room and was walking down the corridor when she bumped into Henry Greenhill. Anyway, he asked her if she was alright, and she said she wanted to get some sleep but was struggling. He said he could get her some Zimovane. Vikki was really shocked."

What's Zimovane?

"But that's a prescription drug," Meed said, frowning. "It's the brand name for zopiclone, something doctors prescribe for short-term insomnia."

"Exactly!" Ellie said triumphantly. "And it gets even worse. Mel walked by us just as Vikki was telling me how she'd said no and fled back to her room. Mel said Henry was just trying to be helpful, and it was well known at Chasingham House that the manager could get guests anything they wanted. She seemed quite proud of it."

Bea's eyes widened. The oh-so-proper manager of the Chasingham was dealing in prescription drugs? Maybe he *was* the one who had stolen the potassium chloride — for a guest maybe? A thought suddenly came into Bea's mind.

What if Greenhill was selling more than stolen prescription drugs? The rich and famous frequented Chasingham House, so he could probably make a killing supplying them with their narcotic of choice. *Oh!* What if Mercy had found out about his sideline? Hadn't Jarvis said she'd disappeared for at least half an hour last night? What if she'd stumbled across Greenhill doing a deal and had threatened to expose him? *He would have a strong motive to kill her...*

"Well, that's interesting," Meed said, opening a notepad and writing something down.

"What's this?" Ellie, standing by the table, held the picture of the jewel up in one hand.

"Oh, it's something that was found on the floor in Mercy's bedroom. We think it could be from a nose stud or maybe an earring," Em told her.

"Or a nail jewel?" Ellie said, walking over and handing the copy of the photo to Claire. "Do you remember Cammy asking Mel this morning if she was going to get her nail fixed? She said she'd noticed at breakfast that Mel had lost the jewel on it."

Claire nodded eagerly. "Yes! And Mel said it was okay as she'd found it and fixed it herself." Claire handed the photo to Meed. "It definitely looks like the one Mel has on one of her index fingers."

"But you said she'd found it, so this can't be hers," Em pointed out.

"Ah, but she could have some spares with her," Perry said. "You buy them in packs, don't you?"

Ellie nodded.

Bea's head was spinning. Mel had keys to her father's suite, so she could have taken the potassium chloride. She'd lost a jewel from her nail and one had been found in Mercy's bedroom. *And* she'd been living in New York at the same time as Mercy. *This is all adding up...* She stifled a groan. Surely not Mel. She was a friend of Flick's and Cammy's. She couldn't be a murderer, could she?

A loud *beep* made her start. DS Meed grabbed his phone from the table and read the message. He jumped up. "Rivers is on his way back. There's been a development."

Bea's stomach did a somersault.

"Well?" Em asked while they all stared at the young sergeant.

"Mel Parks has just been detained. She was caught letting herself into her father's rooms carrying the missing bottle of potassium chloride."

18

3:15 PM, SATURDAY 13 MARCH

"So what happens now?" Perry asked Em as the door slammed shut behind DS Meed. He rose from his chair and walked across the suite, then placed his used cup on the table.

Em shrugged. "They'll interview her to find out why she took it and what she used it for."

"Will they arrest her?" Ellie asked.

Em shook her head. "Not unless she admits she did something illegal. She may have a perfectly reasonable explanation about why she borrowed it from her father's suite."

Bea frowned. *Borrowed it? But surely she... Hold on.* Em was right. Mel had a key that had been given to her by her father, so technically she had his permission to be in his rooms. But then what about—

"But there's the nail jewel!" Claire cried. "We know Mel lost a nail jewel, and one was found in Mercy's bedroom."

"It might not be Mel's," Em said, an edge of frustration creeping into her voice. "And even if it does turn out to be hers, it could have dropped off earlier in the evening when Mel and Vikki took Mercy up to her room."

Bea's mouth was dry. She swallowed. So they had

nothing on Mel. She sighed. *Thank goodness.* She returned to her theory about Greenhill. She really should mention it to Em. *Not all my theories have been bad ones in the past, have they?* And anyway, Em wasn't Fitzwilliam. At least not like the Fitzwilliam she'd used to know. Recently, he'd appeared to mellow somewhat. She smiled. The boorish and arrogant man she'd first been faced with was now kinder, more thoughtful, and seemed to appreciate her input. He was actually quite—

"So what shall we do?" Perry asked, forcing Bea's attention back into the here and now.

"There's nothing we *can* do, Perry," Em said, her shoulders sagging. "We're right back where we started. Without confirmation Mercy was murdered, we can do nothing more. And"—she looked at her watch—"the autopsy report will be a few hours yet. I suggest we go to the pool and relax for a little while. Meed will keep me informed."

"I'm up for that," Claire said, jumping up from her seat.

"Me too," Ellie said, grabbing her room key from the table in front of her. "We'll see you down there."

"Okay," Perry said, heading for the bathroom. "I'll get into my swimming stuff. I won't be a minute."

Bea hesitated. Should she say anything to Em now about her Greenhill-is-a-drug-dealer theory? The more she thought about it, the crazier it seemed. Would Em laugh at her and dismiss her idea as far-fetched? Fitzwilliam had had no bones in the past about telling her she was making wild accusations without any evidence. A shiver ran down her spine when she remembered the time she'd burst into his office during a murder investigation at Francis Court and had informed him very confidently—and rather snootily—that the Francis Court head housekeeper Mrs Crammond had been the murderer, only for him to have gleefully shot her down by informing her that her so-called killer had had an alibi for the time of death. Heat rose up her neck. Did she want to risk that happening again?

Come on, Bea. It's worth a shot.

"Er, Em. Can I run something by you?" she said, then held her breath.

———

The soft ripple of water lapped against the tiled edges of the pool, casting shimmering reflections on the ceiling of Chasingham House's spa complex. Lounging on a plush sunbed, Bea smiled at how worried she'd been earlier to tell Em of her concerns about Greenhill. Em had been receptive to her theory and hadn't once given her the impression she'd thought it was too wild or unbelievable. She'd promised to look into it with Meed. *I can see why Fitzwilliam values her as a friend as well as a colleague.*

Bea scanned the faces of those around her. Wrapped in a white fluffy robe, Perry was excitedly recounting his wedding plans to Claire and Ellie. Beside him sat Claire, looking different without her signature red glasses perched on her nose as she listened intently to Perry.

"You simply must have peonies, Perry," Ellie chimed in. Her highlighted brown hair cascaded down the back of her robe. "They're in season and would look great with roses."

Em's trendy afro bounced around her face as she dipped her head in agreement. "Peonies are beautiful. Izzy and I had them at our wedding too," she added, leaning back comfortably on her lounger.

A warmth spread through Bea's chest. There was something truly magical about being surrounded by people who genuinely cared for one another. She glanced over at Perry, his eyes sparkling as he discussed the flowers that would adorn the Orangery at Francis Court. She had a sudden urge to get up and envelop him in a big hug.

Perry caught her eye and beamed. "Bea, what do you think?" he asked.

Hooking a strand of her long red hair behind her ear, she smiled. "I agree with Ellie and Em. Peonies would complement the roses beautifully."

"Thank you, everyone." Perry grinned, his blue eyes crinkling at the corners. "I'll talk to the florist when I get back. Now if only I could get everything else sorted as easily."

"Like what?" Claire asked, her brown eyes widening with curiosity.

"The table plans. The wedding favours. There's so much still to do!" Perry exclaimed, rubbing his temples in mock exasperation.

"Age-old advice, Perry: don't sweat the small stuff. It'll all come together in the end," Ellie reassured him, reaching over to pat his hand gently.

"Besides," Claire added, "you've got all of us to help you, *and* Lady Sarah does this for a living. You'll be fine."

Bea smiled. Claire was right. Bea's sister Lady Sarah Rosdale, who ran all the major events at Francis Court, had been organising weddings for so long now, there was nothing that fazed her. She knew how to make sure they ran smoothly. *Perry and Simon's wedding will be amazing.*

"Look at the time," Ellie said, jumping up. "We've got treatments booked, Claire. We need to get going."

Claire shot up like a bullet. "I'm finally going to get my age-reducing facial!"

The two women left the poolside and headed to the exit while Perry and Em got into the pool. Bea turned her attention to the group of three women sitting just to her left.

"Cammy, darling, I absolutely adore those sunglasses!" Flick gushed, reaching out to touch the delicate gold frames perched on Cammy's nose. "They're very...avant-garde."

"Why, thank you," Cammy replied, smiling. "I picked them up at a boutique in Paris last month. You know how much I love my accessories."

Flick smiled, her blue eyes flashing. "You'll have to take me shopping next time we're both there."

"Of course, hun. A shopping spree is long overdue," Cammy agreed, her fingers idly playing with a lock of her dark hair.

"Have you seen the latest literary sensation Vikki's representing?" Flick asked, her voice tinged with excitement. "I've read it, and it's impossible to put down!"

"Ah, yes," Vikki replied, smiling at her friend. "It's already been optioned for a film adaptation."

"It will make a great film," Flick said, resting her hand gently on Vikki's arm.

Bea smiled. It was good to see that whatever the issue had been between the two friends, it was now resolved. In fact, the whole group seemed in good spirits.

"Anyone up for a dip in the pool?" Cammy asked, her perfectly proportioned figure in a black one-piece swimming costume causing a slight ripple of envy in Bea's heart. She pulled her robe closer around her. She felt flimsy next to such perfection.

Flick glanced at Vikki, who shook her head. "Later. Right now, I'm going to read."

Cammy raised a perfectly sculpted eyebrow at Flick, who said, "I have a treatment soon."

As a smiling Cammy made her way towards the water, Vikki picked up her book. Flick looked over at Bea. She smiled and rose.

"Mind if I join you, Beatrice?" Flick asked with a smile, gesturing to the empty chair beside Bea.

"Of course not," Bea responded warmly.

Flick settled into the chair, stretching her legs out and sighing contentedly. For a moment, they sat in companionable silence, broken only by the splashing coming from the pool.

Flick cleared her throat. "I was thinking, shall we all meet in the bar tonight before dinner, say six-thirty, and raise a glass to Mercy?"

Bea smiled. "Indeed. I think that's a great idea."

Flick sighed. "I do feel guilty though, you know," she said, watching the others in the water, her voice softer than before. "Poor Mercy is dead, and here we are enjoying ourselves."

"I know what you mean," Bea replied. "But, on the other hand, there's nothing to be done about it. We may as well be here as anywhere else."

"Yes, you're right. But I can't tell you how relieved I'll be when they get to the bottom of her death. We're beginning to think the police think one of us killed her, what with all those questions about where we were and who we were with." Her gaze darted over to where Vikki was lounging, her book held high above her face. As if sensing her friend's eyes on her, she turned her head slightly and gave Flick a slow smile.

Bea's brow creased. *What's going on with these two? They know something.* She was sure of it. She had a hunch. "Mr Greenhill told me he saw someone dressed in black going down the stairs after everyone had gone to bed." Flick's eyes widened as she stared back at Bea. "It was about quarter past eleven between the third and second floor."

Flick's cheeks flamed as she averted her eyes.

Bea's pulse quickened. *I knew it!* "Flick?" Bea whispered, leaning towards her.

Flick glanced at her sideways, her expression wary. "If I tell you, will you promise not to say anything?" Her voice was low and urgent.

Now what do I say? She wanted to agree, but if it was important to the case, she would have to tell Em, wouldn't she? She mentally shook her head. *That's a future problem...* "Of course," she replied in hushed tones.

Flick let out a deep sigh. "It was me."

Bingo!

"I was on my way to Vikki's room; she's on the second floor," Flick continued in a soft voice. She bowed her head, her hair falling around her like a shield. "I...I needed to talk to her," she mumbled.

Bea pressed her lips together. *What's the big deal?* Why had she lied to the police about going to see her friend? "Why lie about it?"

Flick lifted her eyes. "I stayed the night," she hissed.

Oh? Oh... Warmth whooshed up her neck. "You and Vikki are—"

Flick glanced over at her school friend absorbed in her book, then turned back to Bea, a secret smile playing on her lips. "It's been bubbling up for a while, I think. In fact, I've always found her attractive, you know, but then I married Barney, and I sort of buried it. I loved her as a friend and that seemed enough." She reached out and grabbed the sleeve of Bea's robe. "I love my husband. You know him. He's a good man, Beatrice. But Barney and I... Well, I told him right from the start, even before we got married, that I didn't want children, and he said he was fine with that. But he's been a bit down for quite a while, and eventually I asked him why. He admitted he'd only agreed with me about not having children because he believed I would change my mind. But I can't." She shook her head slowly, a wistful look in her eyes. "I told him I needed some space to think and he agreed. I think deep down he already knows we're done. Poor Barney." She let go of Bea's robe and ran her hand through her long thin hair. "He'll make such a great dad." Her voice dropped to a whisper, "So that's why I've decided to let him go."

She wiped away a tear that was trickling down her cheek, then sighed. "I've been talking to Vikki about it, of course. She's been really supportive. She loves Barney too. She never once tried to influence me, but when I told her last night I'd made my decision...well...it all just came out, and it turns out we feel the same way about each other." She gave Bea a shy smile.

Bea's stomach clenched. So Flick had cheated on Barney with Vikki? She pressed her lips tightly together. Flick hadn't seemed like the type to have an affair. *Maybe I don't know her as well as I thought?* What else was she capable of?

Flick's eyes widened. "Bea, we didn't do anything...you know, like that. We were just talking all night. I wouldn't cheat on Barney." She swallowed hard. "It's not his fault..." she mumbled.

Bea's mouth went dry. *Thank goodness.* She hadn't wanted to believe her friends would do such a thing however strongly they felt about each other.

Bea started as Flick caught hold of her sleeve again. "We haven't told anyone yet. Vikki and I won't progress things between us until I tell Barney our marriage is over. You understand, don't you?"

As long as they are honest with each other, who am I to judge? Bea gave her a reassuring smile. "Indeed." *Maybe once Barney is over the shock, he will have a chance to meet someone who also wants children.*

"It wasn't planned, you know. But I'm so happy. I can't tell you...I feel like I can be me now." Flick gave a contented sigh as she removed her hand, then glanced at her watch. She frowned. "Where's Mel? We're both having pedicures in five minutes."

This is awkward. Do I tell her Mel's with the police or—

A low *beep* came from the mobile lying next to Flick on the sunbed. She flipped it over and looked down at the screen. She gasped. "Oh my..." She trailed off as she stared at the phone. She snatched it and scrambled up. "Excuse me, Beatrice. We'll see you in the bar later."

She rushed over to Vikki. "Mel's being interviewed by the police, Vik," she cried. Vikki jumped up. "What?" She began gathering her things together.

Bea strained to hear the rest of what was being said by the two women as they hurried towards the exit, Cammy now out of the pool and running after them. But she did catch the two words "lawyer" and "immediately".

Bea huffed. *That doesn't sound good.*

Perry appeared in front of her, dripping on the tiles. "What's that all about?" he asked, watching the three women leave.

"I think they've just found out Mel is with the police again."

"Oh dear," Perry said, pulling a face. He bent down and gathered up his robe. "Well, I have my body wrap now, so I may not see you until later. What's the plan?"

"Drinks in the bar at six-thirty. We're having a toast to Mercy with the others." Depending on what happens with Mel, I suppose.

"Sure, sounds good. I'll let Ellie and Claire know. I'll see you later."

"Enjoy," Bea said to his retreating back as Em swam over

to the edge of the pool near Bea and hoisted herself out of the water.

"That was refreshing!" she said, reaching for her towel and dabbing at her face. She pulled her swimming cap off and shrugged her robe on. "I'm just going to have a shower and wash my hair. I won't be a minute."

Bea nodded as she sipped her water, her gaze drifting over the tranquil pool. The sun was sparkling through the glass roof, casting dappled patterns on the water's surface. A whiff of chlorine filled the air. She sank further into her chair, lulled by the peaceful atmosphere.

The sudden buzz of Em's phone broke the silence. Bea looked up. Em was hurrying towards her. As she arrived, she reached down and plucked the phone off the lounger next to Bea. With a quizzical look on her face, she read the message, then she looked up, her eyes narrowed. "Blast! Meed says Mel has refused to answer any more questions, and her lawyer is on the way."

19

5 PM, SATURDAY 13 MARCH

Bea made her way back to her room, the plush carpet of Chasingham House's corridors muffling her footsteps. The scent of lavender lingered in the air, a soothing balm for her slightly frayed nerves. She turned the brass handle of her door, stepping inside.

After a shower, she rifled through her wardrobe. She needed something simple and elegant. Like Flick, her thoughts were peppered with guilt at carrying on as normal when Mercy was dead.

Come on, Bea, you hardly knew her. Pull yourself together!

With a sigh, she selected a deep-blue fitted shift dress that ended just on her knees and a pair of gold sandals, hoping the outfit would strike the right balance between smart and respectful.

She added some simple gold jewellery and put on her evening watch. She was early. She would sit and read a magazine for a little while; maybe it would relax her. She sank into the luxurious comfort of the sofa in the sitting area of her room. She patted the empty space beside her. *Ah, Daisy...*

Normally her white West Highland terrier would be nestled by her side. Probably asleep. Almost definitely snoring. She missed the little dog and had been reluctant to leave her behind at Francis Court. But the hotel had a strict policy of not allowing dogs in the spa or the restaurant, so it had seemed better not to bring her. And when Fitzwilliam had offered to have Daisy to stay with him for the weekend, it had seemed better than bringing her here and her having to spend most of the time shut in Bea's room. Anyway, the little terrier adored Fitzwilliam, and the feeling appeared to be mutual. *She probably isn't missing me at all!*

With a sigh, she picked up *Country Life* magazine. She flipped through the first few pages before halting when her phone buzzed next to her. She picked it up, squinting at the screen as she read the message from Em.

Adler (Em): *Come to Perry's suite ASAP. There's news. The autopsy report is out.*

Bea's heart quickened. She glanced at herself in the mirror, scrutinising her reflection. Would anyone notice how rattled she felt? Taking a deep breath, she grabbed her phone and strode out of the room, her heart pounding in anticipation.

20

6:05 PM, SATURDAY 13 MARCH

The scent of fresh flowers and beeswax mingled in the air as Bea walked into Perry's luxurious suite at Chasingham House.

"She's here!" Perry cried, jumping up from the plush emerald-green chaise he'd been sitting on. He was the picture of dapper sophistication, wearing a dinner suit with his perfectly styled strawberry-blond hair primed to perfection. His blue eyes sparkled with excitement as he stopped in front of her. "Em wouldn't tell us what she has until you arrived," he whispered, a smidgin of petulance detectable in his voice.

"Sorry. I came as soon as I could," Bea whispered back, following him to join the group now gathered over by the fireplace. Ellie, looking radiant in a tight red dress that hugged her curves, sipped a glass of wine while chatting animatedly with Claire. Claire listened intently, her brown curls bouncing with each nod of her head. Em stood nearby, her petite frame clad in a black fitted suit and a bubblegum-pink T-shirt. She was reading something on her phone.

As Bea approached, Ellie and Claire stopped talking, their expectant expressions moving from Bea to Em.

Perry grabbed two full glasses of red wine from the low coffee table and handed one to Bea. "I think we're going to need these," he said softly as he raised his glass to her.

It was Claire who broke the silence, her curiosity getting the better of her. "So, Em, what's this urgent meeting all about?"

Bea glanced over at Em, whose brown eyes were now serious and focused as she prepared to speak. The room seemed to hold its breath as they all waited for her answer. "It turns out Mercy had a severe allergic reaction to something she drank. So it looks like it was an unfortunate accident after all."

Bea knew she should be relieved someone hadn't killed Mercy, but somehow it seemed almost more tragic this way. One minute she'd been enjoying a cocktail, and the next, she was gone. No reason. It had just happened.

"An accident," Perry repeated, his voice strained. "After all this, Mercy wasn't murdered. She died from something as simple and as cruel as a reaction to a drink!"

Bea's chin descended in a nod, her fingers absently brushing the fabric of her dress. "Indeed." Why was she still not one hundred percent convinced? Perhaps it was because they'd spent so much time suspecting foul play...

"Accidents happen," Claire chimed in, her full lips curved into a sad smile. "I suppose we should be relieved it wasn't something more sinister."

"Relieved?" Ellie scoffed, her large mouth pinched. "A woman is still dead, Claire."

"Of course," Claire said, pushing her glasses up her nose. "I just meant... well, at least no one else is in danger."

Ellie's face softened. "Sorry, you're right." She smiled at Claire apologetically, and her friend returned her smile.

"Was it strawberry?" Perry asked as he stopped his

pacing. He stood with his back to the windows, the sun casting a warm glow across his sharp features.

Em set her phone down on the table with a decisive thud. She glanced at her friends. "I don't know yet. I've just received a text from my contact at the coroner's office. She's sending over a copy of the autopsy report now." She walked over towards where Bea was standing, sank into an armchair, and pulled her laptop from the coffee table onto her lap, flicking the screen upright as she did so.

Bea frowned. Did Em want to see the full report to satisfy her own curiosity? Or did she doubt the conclusion?

Em scanned through the report, her eyebrows knitted together in concentration. The room was silent, the only sound was the ticking of a grandfather clock tucked in the corner of the room.

"According to the report," Em began, her voice steady, "there were no traces of potassium chloride found in Mercy's body."

Bea's shoulders dipped. *That's Mel off the hook then. Thank goodness for that.*

Em continued, "If it had been used, there would have been some trace of it in her system."

So what had Mel wanted with her father's stash of the medicine?

Perry leaned back against the window seat. "So how does Mel taking it fit into everything then?"

"Perhaps it's a red herring," Claire suggested, crossing her legs elegantly. "Or maybe it could be connected to another crime altogether. Something we haven't uncovered yet."

Maybe something to do with Greenhill's sideline in supplying prescription drugs? Was Mel working with the manager on this?

"Here we go," Em said, tapping her finger on her laptop screen. "There was significant lung congestion, diffuse or focal lung emphysema, and a mucus plug in the trachea."

"Yuck!" Perry said, pulling a face.

"It says these symptoms point to anaphylactic shock." Em shook her head. "I've seen this before. The immune system overreacts and floods the body with chemicals, causing it to go into shock. If not treated quickly, then it causes death." She paused, letting the information sink in. "Hold on. Here it is. They found traces of both strawberries *and* mango in the glass in her room."

"So it *was* the strawberry?" Perry asked.

"But she ordered it. Why would she do that if she knew she had an allergy?" Claire interjected, her eyes wide with disbelief. "Surely she would've avoided it like the plague."

Ellie chimed in, her voice soft but steady. "But she may not have known how serious it was. I know from all the food prep training I've done that allergies can come and go, you know. It's possible she'd eaten strawberry in the past but only been mildly affected. She might only have developed a more severe reaction recently. It happens."

Bea stared at Francis Court's catering manager. *Really?* She sighed. The idea that Mercy hadn't known her allergy was life threatening was both sad and frightening. How many others walked through life unaware of such hidden dangers lurking within their own bodies?

Beep. "Hold on." Em picked up her vibrating phone and read something on the screen. Her face fell.

Bea's stomach rolled.

Perry's eyes narrowed. "Something's changed, hasn't it?"

"Yes." Em looked up from her screen, her voice steady despite the sombre expression on her face. "That was DS Meed. He's just spoken to Mercy's parents. They landed in the States a short while ago. It turns out Mercy was allergic to *mango,* and it was severe. She was diagnosed just six weeks ago during a trip to A&E after she'd eaten mango chutney and became very ill."

The room went deathly quiet as the news sank in. Bea could feel her heart pounding in her chest, the implications of Em's words hitting her like a ton of bricks.

"Wait," Claire interjected, her voice trembling slightly. "So you're saying not only did Mercy know she was allergic to mangoes, but she knew they could kill her? And she told no one?"

"Correct," Emma replied, nodding. "Her parents told Meed that she hadn't yet got used to the idea she had a life-threatening condition and was embarrassed to tell anyone. It caused a row, and in the end, her parents agreed to let her tell her friends and work colleagues in her own time. In return, she promised she would carry her allergy card and an EpiPen with her at all times."

Card and EpiPen? So where were they?

"But as we know, we found neither on her when she died."

So that meant her death *hadn't* been an accident; someone had deliberately put mango in her cocktail and taken her EpiPen away so she would die. A shiver ran through Bea's body.

Perry's fingers tapped nervously on the mantelpiece above the fireplace, a pensive look clouding his blue eyes. "So where are they?" he said, breaking the silence.

"And that, Perry, is the million dollar question," Em replied.

"Maybe she just forgot them?" Ellie suggested, though her uncertainty was evident in her voice.

Em looked back down at her phone screen. "The police

are checking her parents' house just to make sure, but her mother told Meed she had double-checked with Mercy before she'd left to come here and that she'd had her card and pen on her."

So someone took it. Bea didn't need to say it out loud. Her friends' faces all said the same thing.

Slipping her phone in her jacket pocket, Em stood. "Now that it's likely Mercy was murdered, I'm going to insist Rivers keeps me officially in the loop this time. He and Meed are due back here any minute."

"What do you need us to do?" Perry said, his jaw set in determination.

"For now, let's keep this between us. No need to alarm anyone else until we know more," Em replied. She looked down at her feet and took a deep breath.

She must be steeling herself to face Rivers.

"I suggest you all go to the bar as planned. See if the other girls knew about the mango allergy but ask discreetly. I don't want to alert them that anything has changed."

Bea tilted her head in a nod, swallowing hard. *In case one of them is the murderer and it tips them off?* She wrapped her arms around herself.

"And I want you to stay vigilant," Em said, her voice subdued. She looked from Perry to Bea and back. "And don't go and do anything silly."

Bea bristled. So Fitzwilliam must have told Em of some of their previous cases where, through no fault of their own, she or Perry had come face to face with a killer. More than once in her case.

"Stay together and watch each other's backs. If you see or hear anything, let me know immediately. I'll be in the downstairs conference room. Agreed?"

They all nodded.

"Alright," Perry said, breaking the silence. "Let's act naturally and try to enjoy the rest of our evening. Oh, and make sure you're not left alone with the killer."

"Hear, hear," Claire said. Raising their glasses, she and Ellie downed their remaining wine in one.

21

6:35 PM, SATURDAY 13 MARCH

As Perry's party entered the bar, the warm glow of the overhead lights reflecting off the polished wooden surfaces created an inviting atmosphere that contrasted sharply with the chilling news they had just heard. The low hum of conversation punctuated by the *clink* of glasses was coming from the corner where a fire crackled merrily, casting flickering shadows across the walls.

"Ah, there they are," Claire said, heading towards Cammy, Flick, and Vikki, who were seated in a cosy nook near the fireplace. Cammy saw them and waved them over with a flourish.

"I'll get the drinks," Perry said to Bea. As he strode off towards the bar, she followed Claire and Ellie. As they took the two chairs next to Vikki and opposite Flick, Bea slid into the booth next to Cammy.

"Where's Em?" Flick asked, her heavily made-up eyes wide with curiosity.

Bea hesitated and glanced hurriedly at Ellie.

"Oh, she had a wardrobe malfunction," Ellie said, pulling

a face that said, 'we've all been there, haven't we, ladies?' "She'll be here a little later."

They nodded sympathetically.

As the conversation flowed around her, Bea noticed Mel was missing. If she was no longer a suspect, why was she not here with the others?

"Where's Mel?" she asked Cammy, who was sipping on a frothy cocktail that matched her vibrant pink dress.

"Her lawyer's still here. I think they're on the phone to her father. He's in the States on business at the moment."

"Speaking of America," Bea said, trying to sound casual, "I've been meaning to ask her about her time in New York. I love it there. Was she there working?"

"Ah, yes, Mel's big New York adventure," Cammy began, her voice taking on a wistful tone. "She went there for a modelling campaign about ten years ago. It was only supposed to be for a few weeks, but she ended up staying when she fell in love with this guy."

"Really? What happened?" Bea asked, her interest piqued.

"Well, it's a sad story, really," Cammy replied, her gaze drifting towards the flickering candle on their table. "She met him at a charity thing. His father was some big shot lawyer with political ambitions. Anyway, he was a lawyer too, working for his father's firm. It was love at first sight according to Mel. I went over there about a month after they'd met, and they seemed madly, truly, deeply, you know. He appeared like a nice guy too. I'd never seen her so happy. Then suddenly she was back in London, and he'd married someone else. Mel was clearly heartbroken, but she wouldn't talk about it. Then just a few months later, she found out Ross had killed himself."

Ross? Bea gasped. Cammy rested her hand on Bea's arm. "I know. So I wouldn't ask her about New York if I was you. I think it's still too painful for her."

Bea felt a chill run down her spine as the weight of Cammy's words sank in. She tried to maintain a composed expression, masking the shock threatening to rise to the surface. "That's…terrible," she managed to say, her voice cracking slightly. "Poor Mel."

"Exactly." Cammy bobbed her head, her eyes clouding over with a mixture of sadness and sympathy. She picked up her drink and took a large gulp. Around them, the others carried on with their conversations, unaware of the sombre turn the discussion between Bea and Cammy had taken. As Bea listened to the hum of voices and the clinking of glassware, she couldn't help but replay Cammy's revelation in her mind.

Ross? Mercy's husband, Ross? That must be the connection between Mel and Mercy! Her chest ached. Mel couldn't be Mercy's killer, could she? She blinked rapidly. *Wait, it could just be a strange coincidence.* Fitzwilliam's face appeared in her mind. He was shaking his head. *Rats!*

She had to tell Em. She glanced around the table, taking in the faces of the others as they remained engrossed in their own conversations. She looked over at the bar. Perry was listening intently to Jarvis Freeth as the barman mixed their drinks. The two men suddenly looked over towards the group. *What are they talking about?* Maybe Perry had found out something useful too?

Right, I need to go. She shuffled along the bench slightly. Cammy looked up and caught her eye.

"Excuse me," Bea said to her, sliding out of the booth and rising to her feet. "I, uh, I just want to check Em's okay."

"Of course," Cammy said, smiling as she sipped her drink. "Tell her it doesn't matter what she's wearing. She needs to come down and start drinking." She raised her glass.

"Indeed," Bea said, offering Cammy a weak wave as she turned on her heels and left the bar.

22

A SHORT WHILE BEFORE, SATURDAY 13 MARCH

Perry scanned the dimly lit cocktail bar, Space, as he left Bea and made his way towards the bar. The warm glow of hanging Edison bulbs illuminated the vintage suitcases repurposed as shelves behind the wooden counter, where rows of colourful bottles stood, their reflections in the mirrors creating a rainbow effect.

"Mr Juke!" Jarvis called out from behind the counter, smiling as he approached.

"Evening, Jarvis," Perry replied, returning the smile as he perched himself on a barstool.

"Just give me a sec," Jarvis said, shaking the cocktail shaker with practiced ease, the ice clinking rhythmically against the stainless steel. He poured the contents of the shaker into a martini glass and garnished it with a green olive on a stick. Placing it on a tray, he moved the tray to the other side of the bar, where a server picked it up and took it away. Jarvis dried his hands on a nearby towel and focused his attention back on Perry. "What can I get you?"

Perry gave him their order of cocktails, and Jarvis nodded

as he picked up another silver cocktail shaker and selected a bottle from the array on the shelf behind him.

Perry leaned over the counter. A tray of cut fruit was laid out just under the bar. Strawberries, oranges, lemon, lime, cucumber, and cherries. *But no mango?* "Where do you keep the mango?"

"Actually, we don't use whole mangoes here." Jarvis decanted the cocktail from the shaker into a tall glass. "They spoil too quickly. I use concentrated mango juice for the magnificent mango moucher, the only cocktail on the menu with mango in it. I top it off with pomegranate seeds and a sprig of mint. Would you like to try one?"

Perry shook his head. "No thanks." *So no knife was used that could have caused cross-contamination.*

Jarvis wiped the condensation off the counter top where he'd been preparing the drinks, then opened the door of a small dishwasher and placed the used cocktail shaker inside. He shut the door and grabbed a clean shaker from the shelf above him.

Jarvis obviously keeps the area clean and doesn't re-use shakers. The chances of this being an accident seemed to be getting slimmer.

Jarvis poured two shots of a clear liquid and one of a lime-green coloured liqueur into the shaker, then added a large scoop of ice. He twisted on the top and began to shake.

"Did you know Mercy Bright was allergic to mango, Jarvis?"

Jarvis stopped, his eyes wide. He set down the shaker he was holding, the cold metal making a hollow sound as it hit the top of the bar. His face paled. "Jeez, is that what killed her?"

Perry nodded.

Jarvis let go of the shaker and scraped his fingers through his short brown hair. "Am I in trouble?"

He looks genuinely shocked, Perry thought, giving him a reassuring smile. "You weren't to know."

Jarvis reached out and grabbed the sleeve of Perry's jacket. "But I did know."

Perry's mind raced, trying to decipher what this revelation might mean. If Jarvis had known about the allergy, could he be the killer? But then why would he willingly admit to knowing such crucial information? *That would be stupid.* "How did you know?"

"She came up to the bar when she first arrived and asked me if we had any mango-based cocktails. When I said yes, she asked me to be extra careful not to let any mango near her drinks as she had an allergy to it." A frown creased his brow as he added, "At the time, I didn't think it was a life-threatening allergy, of course, and she certainly didn't tell me it was."

He picked up the cocktail shaker again and resumed shaking. He deftly poured the now vibrant green liquid from inside into a tall glass, topped it with crushed ice, and finished it off with a sprig of mint. As he put it on a tray, he said, "I was ultra careful. I swear."

"I'm sure you were," Perry replied quickly, not wanting Jarvis to feel accused. *At least not yet...* "Did you tell the police?"

Jarvis shook his head. "No. They didn't ask, and I didn't think to say. They just told me she was dead and asked about that evening and who was where. It didn't cross my mind it was relevant."

Is he telling the truth? Perry was inclined to think so. The young man looked genuinely worried. His hands trembled slightly as he wiped down the bar counter, a faraway look in his eyes. Perry felt a pang of sympathy for him; he wanted to reassure Jarvis he wasn't to blame. But how could he without revealing Mercy had been murdered?

"Jarvis," Perry said gently, leaning towards him. "I believe you when you say you were careful, so please don't worry."

"Thank you," Jarvis replied, managing a small smile. "But there is one thing," he continued, anxiety creeping into his voice as he set the towel aside. He glanced around nervously. "I was here on Friday afternoon," he said, his voice barely a whisper. "I served Mrs Bright a glass of champagne, then I went to the back to cut up fruit for the drinks. The door to the bar was open, and I overheard her talking with someone."

Perry's eyes widened slightly, but he kept his composure. He watched Jarvis intently, his mind already sifting through possible implications of this new information. *Whoever it was could be our killer!* He leaned forward onto the bar. "Who was it?"

Jarvis scratched his head, a crease forming on his brow. "I didn't see. I just heard their voices," Jarvis said, an apologetic tone in his voice.

Perry's stomach plummeted. He'd so wanted to be the one to provide Em with something that would lead them directly to Mercy's murderer.

"The woman asked her if she'd decided what cocktail to have later. Mrs Bright said she liked the look of the strawberry sensation. The other woman said she wanted to try the magnificent mango moucher. That's when Mrs Bright told her she had an allergy to mango so would be keeping away from that one."

"Would you recognise the voice if you heard it again?" Perry pressed, his heart thudding with anticipation.

Jarvis glanced over towards where Bea, Ellie, and Claire were talking to Cammy, Flick, and Vikki by the fireplace, their voices rippling through the room like the warm glow of the fire. "It was definitely one of those posh ladies."

Perry followed Jarvis' gaze. His mind raced, trying to piece together the puzzle. Cammy, Flick, or Vikki. He paused. But if the tall woman seen by Greenhill was also the killer, then that narrowed it down further to Flick or Cammy.

Just then Bea stood. She waved her hand at Cammy and turned to walk away. *Where's she going?* He watched her hurry out of the room. *Maybe she's got something interesting too...*

He jumped down from the barstool. "Well, thanks, Jarvis. Try not to—"

"But don't you want to know who had the magnificent mango moucher? I'm not sure if it was the same lady talking to Mrs Bright, but..." Jarvis trailed off, a look of embarrassment across his face.

Perry clutched the side of the stool to steady himself. "Who?"

23

MEANWHILE, SATURDAY 13 MARCH

"So, chief inspector, what's your next move?" Em faced Rivers across the conference table, a glint in her eyes. She could tell he didn't want to play nice with her, but now that Mercy's death was most likely a murder case, he had no choice. A member of the royal family could be in danger; he couldn't afford to keep things from her now.

"Well, *chief inspector*," Rivers sneered, "I don't think that's any of your business."

But he was clearly going to be as awkward as he could.

Em sighed. "Do I have to remind you that in the case of a murder investigation involving a member of the royal family, you are obliged to keep me in the—"

Rivers held up his hand in front of her face. Em stopped, her pulse skyrocketing. *How dare he!*

"This is not a murder investigation *yet*." Rivers lowered his hand and tilted his head to the side. "We don't know for sure Mercy Bright was killed deliberately. We have no physical evidence to support a murder claim. No fingerprints. No DNA. No fibres. Nothing. All we know is that she drank something with mango in it. Fact."

"But someone took her card and EpiPen. Why would anyone do that unless they—"

Again the hand came up. Em swallowed hard. "We don't know she even had them with her." Rivers said, smirking.

"But…but…her mother," Em spluttered. *What's wrong with this man?*

Rivers dropped his arm and shrugged. "She *thinks* her daughter may have had them with her. But she's far from sure. I wouldn't be surprised if we get a call soon to say she's found them in Mercy's room at home." He rose, and resting his hands on the desk, he leaned towards her. The heady blend of aromatic and amber notes in his aftershave hit Em's nostrils. Her face puckered. "Let me tell you what I think happened. I think Mercy was too embarrassed to tell anyone she had a severe allergy to mango. I mean, it's a bit silly, isn't it, to be allergic to a fruit. So she said nothing. She had too much to drink. She picked up someone else's cocktail. She took it upstairs. She drank it. She collapsed. She died. It was an accident."

Em's stomach clenched. Did he really believe it was that simple? *The man's an idiot!* "But I've read Vikki's statement. She says Mercy was drinking the strawberry sensation cocktail, and that's what she took up with her," she pointed out.

Rivers pulled one hand from the table and waved it dismissively in the air. "That's just her opinion. Maybe the bartender made a mistake. He's only a young lad. Either way, the lab results say there was mango in her glass as well as strawberry."

"Because someone put it there!" Em could barely keep the frustration out of her voice. "And what about the woman Mr Greenhill saw around the time Mercy died? Are you just going to ignore that?"

Rivers gave an exaggerated sigh. "Probably a guest

sneaking off to meet up with a secret lover." He wiggled his eyebrows. Em felt sick.

He straightened up and rubbed his hands together. "Look," he said, suddenly sounding weary. "No one knew her apart from Vikki Carrington, and even she didn't know her that well. We've done background checks on all the guests and the staff. There is nothing to connect any of them to Mercy. There is no motive for murder, Ms Adler." He shrugged and held up his hands..

Em slouched back in her seat. She hated to admit it, but he did have a point. She stifled a groan. Had she got so carried away with trying to prove a point to him that she'd convinced herself Mercy's death was murder when it had simply been an accident?

The door opened, and DS Meed walked in. "Sir. Ma'am. Miss Parks' lawyer is getting quite vocal. He insists we have no right to keep his client here against her will. He's advising her to pack up her things and leave with him immediately."

Em rose. "Sergeant. Did Mel Parks give a reason why she had her father's potassium chloride in her possession?"

Meed shook his head. "She refused to say. By the time her lawyer arrived, we had the autopsy results, and it was no longer relevant."

What had Mel been up to? *Was it something to do with Greenhill and his prescription scam?* Was Bea right — had Mercy found out and threatened to expose them?

Meed cleared his throat. "Sir?" Rivers, who had been gazing out of the window, turned, a bored expression on his face. "What should I tell him?"

"Yes, yes. Well, technically he's right. We really have no good reason to keep any of the guests here if they want to leave. Tell him everyone will be free to go in the morning."

Em blinked. *Let them go?* But they hadn't heard from Mercy's parents yet. It could still be—

"Off you go, sergeant," River barked.

Meed gave her a short apologetic smile, then turned and left.

"Now, chief inspector. Don't you think you'd better go and check up on your charge just in case—"

Suddenly the door burst open and Adler's 'charge' came storming in. "Em, I think I know who killed Mercy!" Bea cried as she rushed towards her.

24

A FEW SECONDS LATER, SATURDAY
13 MARCH

Bea's heart pounded in her chest as she stopped at the top of the oak table that occupied most of the space in the conference room. Standing either side of the table glaring at each other were Em and DCI Rivers.

Rivers turned to stare at her, a sour look on his face while Em stood opposite him, her arms crossed. *Oh dear, I think I might have interrupted something. And he already doesn't like me. Great!*

Em uncrossed her arms and smiled weakly at Bea. "Lady Beatrice, you know Detective Chief Inspector Rivers from Chase Police." Em held her arm out in the direction of the policeman.

Head down, Rivers grunted as he gave a short bow in Bea's direction. Bea tried to catch his eye and smile, but he wasn't playing ball. *Well, if you're going to be like that...* She dropped her arm. "I'm sorry to burst in like this." She gave Em a hesitant smile.

"Of course, my lady. Please take a seat," Em said rather formally.

Bea glanced around the small room, taking in the worn

leather chairs and the faint scent of lavender that seemed to cling to everything at Chasingham House. She pulled out the nearest chair, then shifted her focus back to Em and Rivers. The tension between them crackled like static as they both sat. *Well, this is awkward.* "Er, I have some information that might be useful."

Rivers' bushy eyebrows shot up over his black-rimmed glasses. He looked like a disgruntled owl as he crossed his arms over his tweed jacket. "Oh? And what might that be?"

"Mel Parks," Bea blurted out, feeling the warmth of a blush on her cheeks. "I think she had a motive to kill Mercy." Walking to the conference room to find Em, it had pained Bea to reluctantly accept that Mel was most likely Mercy's killer.

The sharp twist of Rivers' mouth made it clear he wasn't pleased with Bea's involvement in his case. "And how did you come by this information?" he sneered.

"Never mind that now," Em interjected. She leaned towards Bea, her brown eyes shining. "What's the connection between Mel and Mercy, my lady?"

"I think Mercy's husband Ross was Mel's ex-boyfriend," Bea said, her voice shaky at first but growing stronger. "If so, he left her for Mercy, then died two months later. Mel's never got over it."

"How did you find out?" Em asked gently, and Bea recounted what Cammy had told her. Em raised an eyebrow, clearly intrigued. "That's a clear connection and would give Mel a motive, certainly. We know from the background we've done that Mel was in New York at the same time as Mercy. All we need to do now is a bit of digging about Ross and—"

"Absolutely not!" Rivers burst out, slamming his palm down on the table. Bea jumped. He turned to glare at her.

"Lady Beatrice, you should not be snooping around and talking to suspects. This is a police investigation!"

Bea dropped his gaze and looked at the table. *Rats! I should have waited until Em was on her own.*

"An investigation into a death you've just told me is merely an accident?" Em retorted sharply. "So by your logic, there are no suspects, are there?"

You tell him, Em! Bea's mouth dropped open slightly as Em locked eyes with Rivers, a silent battle of wills unfolding between them.

"Regardless." Rivers scoffed, adjusting his glasses. "She shouldn't be interfering in police matters."

Bea shifted in her seat. She suppressed a grin. *Rivers is making Fitzwilliam look like a pussy cat.*

"Is this how PaIRS runs things?" Rivers sniped, his large nose wrinkling with disdain. "Getting members of the royal family to spy on people?"

Em's jaw tightened. She looked poised to launch a scathing retort.

That's enough; we're straying from the point. Bea cleared her throat. "DCI Rivers," she said in her best lady-of-the-manor voice. "I can assure you, my connection to the royal family has nothing to do with my desire to help."

Rivers gave a heavy sigh, then pressed his lips together into a fine line.

Ignoring Rivers' indignation, Bea pressed on, her voice firm and steady. "And regardless of how I obtained the information, Mel has a motive to kill Mercy. That's what matters."

The air in the small conference room fizzed with tension as if it were charged with electricity. Bea could practically taste the animosity radiating from Rivers, who leaned back in his chair and puffed out his chest. "So she has a motive. But where's the actual evidence connecting Mel Parks to Mercy's death?"

Bea opened her mouth, but no words came out. Rivers was right; they had no solid proof linking Mel to the crime, only her suspicions and a gut feel she was on the right path.

"Just as I thought," he said pompously, adjusting his tweed jacket as he stood up. "I have other matters to attend to. You ladies can go back to your—"

The door opened with a *whoosh*, and Perry came flying in. The door slammed behind him. "I know who killed Mercy," he cried, his blue eyes shining with excitement.

25

A FEW MORE SECONDS LATER,
SATURDAY 13 MARCH

The door to the small conference room at Chasingham House had slammed open with such force, Bea had jumped out of her seat. As Perry, his spiky blond hair practically vibrating with excitement, made his way towards them, she lowered herself down again. His blue eyes were wide, and his breathing was shallow.

"Sorry to interrupt!" Perry blurted as he put one hand on his hip and the other on the side of the table. "But I've found out something important!"

About to open his mouth to continue, he was beaten to it by an outraged looking Rivers. "Another one of your friends who's been snooping around, Ms Adler?" Rivers shot daggers at Em. "You really do have a penchant for involving civilians in my investigation," he said incredulously, his bushy eyebrows shooting up towards his bald dome of a head.

Perry's eyes darted to Bea's face as he removed his hand from the table and straightened his well-tailored dinner jacket. He gave a barely perceptible nod in the direction of Rivers and Em, who were glaring at each other across the table. Bea raised her eyebrows. *They don't seem to be seeing eye to eye.* He gave her a quick smile, and she could see the determination in his piercing blue eyes. Whatever Perry had uncovered was important.

"Well, never mind that," Em said, her voice taking on a steely edge. She focused on Perry, her brown eyes glinting with curiosity. "What have you found out, Perry?"

"Before I say anything," Perry said, his voice carrying a hint of nerves despite his confident posture. He held Rivers' eye as he continued, "I want you to know I wasn't *snooping.* I was just asking Jarvis a few questions."

"Jarvis Freeth, the bartender?" Em asked.

Perry nodded.

"Just get to the point," Rivers snapped, his patience clearly wearing thin.

Perry shifted uncomfortably under Rivers' unyielding gaze but held his ground. "Alright." He pouted and rolled his shoulders back. "Jarvis overheard Mercy telling someone on Friday about her allergy to mangoes. He didn't actually see who she was talking to because he was in the back of the bar, but he remembered who ordered the magnificent mango moucher."

Bea's stomach bunched into a knot. *Who?*

"And who was it?" Em asked.

"Mel Parks!"

Bea's eyes widened as she processed this new information, her mind racing with possibilities. Mel had known about Mercy's allergy. *It isn't looking good for Mel.*

Rivers' face turned a shade of crimson. It was obvious the DCI was struggling to contain his anger at the unwelcome assistance from first her, then Perry. He clenched his fists, his knuckles whitening, and he took a deep breath as though willing himself to remain calm. "Look," he growled through gritted teeth, "I appreciate that you all want to help, but this is a police investigation, not an amateur detective club."

"Rivers, stop being so obstructive and think about it," Em interjected in a steely voice. "We may have just uncovered crucial information. Mel had both motive and knowledge of Mercy's allergy. Don't you think it's worth exploring?" When he said nothing, she gave him a pointed look. "Did Mel tell you in her statement that she didn't know about Mercy's allergy?" she asked.

The muscles in Rivers' jaw tightened, but he nodded reluctantly. "Er… Yes."

"Then she lied!" Perry cried, his blue eyes flashing with conviction. "If Jarvis overheard her talking about it on Friday, then she must have known *before* Mercy died!"

"However," Rivers snapped, his voice as sharp as a scalpel. "That still isn't enough." He tapped his fingers on the table, leaning in as if to emphasise his point. "There's no concrete evidence linking Mel to the crime, and she has an alibi."

"An alibi?" Perry asked, his brows furrowed.

Bea's stomach clenched. *Of course. She was attending an online webinar.* How had she forgotten that?

"She was attending an online webinar during the time of Mercy's death," Rivers said, leaning back and folding his arms across his chest.

Bea's heart sank like a punctured balloon. She twirled the rings on her right hand. She was so sure it was Mel. Bea's mind raced. *There must be something we're missing.* She glanced over at Perry, but his head was down, his foot tracing a slow circle on the carpeted floor. *How did she do it?* "Maybe she logged on, then left it running?"

Rivers shrugged dismissively. "I doubt it."

Bea felt her blood rising. "Can't you at least find out if it's possible?"

"Or perhaps, my lady," Rivers said sharply, "you should leave the detective work to the professionals. This is all circumstantial. So she *may* have had a motive. So she *may* have known Mercy was allergic to mango. She *may* even have not really been on that webinar. So what? It doesn't mean she killed her. In fact, we don't have any evidence Mercy was even killed. This is a waste—"

The door to the conference room burst open, and DS Meed strode in. "Sorry to interrupt, but I have news," he announced.

26

STRAIGHT AFTER, SATURDAY 13 MARCH

"Come in and join the party, sergeant," Rivers said sarcastically as he gestured for Meed to approach the table in the conference room at Chasingham House. "Out with it then, man," Rivers commanded.

Bea held her breath, hoping against hope Meed had come bearing the breakthrough they so desperately needed. Perry, who had now moved to sit next to her, whispered, "He's so rude!" Bea inclined her head in agreement.

"Er, yes. Sorry, sir. So when we discovered Mel Parks had taken the potassium chloride but before we found out Mercy had died from a reaction to mango, I attempted to verify Miss Parks' alibi."

Bea sucked in a deep breath. Was Mel's alibi about to be blown out of the water?

"I didn't ask you to do that!" Rivers barked.

Meed glanced at Em. *Had she asked him?*

"Well, I think that shows initiative, sergeant. Why don't you tell us what you found," Em said, giving him a reassuring smile.

"I discovered that the webinar Miss Parks claimed to have

been attending on Friday evening was actually a pre-recorded session." He paused, looking at Rivers, then continued, "It means she could have easily watched it at any time, and her alibi is no longer as solid as we initially believed."

"Another lie!" Perry said, his voice rising with indignation. "She must be guilty!"

He could be right. Mel had a motive and now no alibi. Just as Bea shot Em a look, the door burst open once more, admitting a whirlwind of energy in the form of Claire and Ellie.

"We have new information!" Claire cried, her curly brown hair bouncing as she waved her arms dramatically.

Ellie nodded vigorously. Her blue eyes sparkled with excitement behind her wispy fringe. "You won't believe what we've just found out."

Bea's heart skipped a beat. Did they have something that would prove once and for all who'd done it?

Rivers' face turned an alarming shade of red, the veins bulging at his temples. "You've all been talking to suspects? Unbelievable!" he shouted, slamming his fist on the table. "Do you have any idea how much you're jeopardising this investigation?"

Ellie and Claire stopped and stood still. Their faces registered confusion as they looked from Em to Rivers and back.

Em, her eyes narrowing, shot back, "Shut up and listen, Rivers! They might have found something vital to the investigation!" She looked away from Rivers before he could respond. "Tell us what you've learned."

Claire took a deep breath, her red glasses perched precariously on her nose, threatening to slip off at any moment. "Well, as you know, we were just at the bar with the other girls, and after Bea left, I got to chatting with Cammy. I noticed she'd had her nails done, so—"

"Her nails?" Rivers interrupted, his voice dripping with sarcasm. "Really? This is the important information you're bringing me? She's had her nails done?"

"So rude!" Perry murmured beside Bea.

It was clear Rivers' patience wad at its upper limit, but Bea sensed that whatever Claire and Ellie were about to reveal might be significant. She'd better say something to him—

"Listen!" Claire snapped, a fierce determination in her eyes as she gave Rivers a withering look. "It's important!"

Bea stifled a giggle. Claire could obviously handle herself.

"Alright then," Rivers grumbled, though his body language still radiated skepticism.

"Right, her nails," Claire continued, clearly pleased to have River's attention again. "You see, she had these little jewels on each of her index fingers. She said she was inspired by Mel's nails, which she'd had done at the spa here on Friday afternoon."

Rivers huffed in annoyance, but Ellie turned and shushed him firmly. Bea felt her pulse quicken. She was trying to connect the dots between their observations and the murder investigation.

Claire continued, "Unfortunately, Cammy was saying she'd already lost one of the jewels by the time she'd finished getting dressed this evening. She rang Mel in her room for some advice, and Mel had a kit with her and fixed it for her just before we met up tonight. It wasn't an exact match, but it's close enough."

"Close enough," Bea murmured, her thoughts racing ahead of the conversation. "Claire, did either the original jewel or the replacement one look like the photo of the one that was found in Mercy's room?"

"Yes, the original one—"

Rivers exploded from his chair. "What do you mean, photo? How did you see a photo of the crime scene?" He slammed his hands on the table and leaned towards Em. "Did you share photos of—"

"Sir!" Meed's voice was loud enough to get everyone's attention. Rivers spun around to face the sergeant. Meed cleared his throat, then said in a calm voice, "I think we should hear them out, sir."

The two men stared at each other for a moment while Bea held her breath. Then Rivers sat down. "Alright," Rivers said reluctantly, adjusting the glasses that had slid down his nose. "But what does this have to do with Mercy's death?"

"That's what she's about to tell you," Ellie hissed.

Claire turned to Em. "Remember how Ellie and I overheard Cammy asking Mel about the jewel she'd lost from her nail, and Mel said she'd found it?" Em nodded. Rivers shifted in his seat. Meed gave a wry smile.

"Well, I said to Cammy it was really useful that Mel had some spare jewels, and I asked her if Mel had lost one as well. Cammy, of course, said yes. She'd noticed at breakfast on Saturday morning that one of Mel's jewels was missing. I wondered out loud when she'd lost it. I suggested Mel might have lost it during the evening, but Cammy said no, it was still on her nail when they'd all gone up to bed."

"*After* Mel had come back from taking Mercy up to her room with Vikki!" Ellie cried triumphantly.

Bea's heart skipped a beat. *So Mel must have dropped it in Mercy's room later? When she went up to—*

"Oh my giddy aunt!" Perry cried out from beside her. "She must have dropped it when she went up to kill her."

27

AND THEN... SATURDAY 13 MARCH

Perry's statement hung in the air like a heavy mist. In the silence that followed, Bea scanned the room. Em fidgeted with the hem of her T-shirt while Perry, his arms folded, looked a bit like a disgruntled James Bond. Claire's face was uncharacteristically serious as she adjusted her red glasses, and Ellie stood tall, radiating determination. DS Meed hovered next to them at the end of the table. All eyes were on DCI Rivers, who was still sitting opposite Em, his lips pinched tightly, a thunderous look on his face as he eyed the group warily.

Em shifted in her seat, crossed her arms, and lifted her chin defiantly. "Well, at the very least, you should interview Mel," she said, her voice steady and assertive. "See what she has to say about all this."

Rivers let out a short, humourless laugh. "I appreciate your input, Ms Adler, but I'll remind you that this is my investigation, not yours." He cast a stern look around the room, addressing them all. "All you've brought me is speculation and supposition. We still don't know for sure Mercy Bright was murdered."

Bea felt her frustration rise. Gripping her hands tightly, she took a deep breath before speaking. "But everything seems to point to Mel being in Mercy's room when she shouldn't have been. Surely that's enough to at least investigate further?"

"Hear, hear!" Perry mumbled beside her.

"And you're basing that on what? The nail jewel found in her room? For all we know, that could have come from someone else — a maid or a previous guest, perhaps."

"But Mel lied about having an alibi for the time of death, Rivers," Em pointed out.

Rivers raked a hand through his hair, his expression one of exasperation as he addressed her. "May I remind you she isn't the only one without an alibi."

Bea's brow furrowed. That wasn't entirely accurate. Cammy had been on the phone to her boyfriend, and Vikki and Flick had been together. Mel was the *only* one of the birthday girls without an alibi. She stifled a groan. But, of course, she couldn't say anything as she'd promised Flick, and Claire had promised Cammy, that they wouldn't tell anyone. *What about...* "Motive!" she blurted out. "Mel had a reason to want to hurt Mercy. She's the only one who seems to have a connection that runs deeper than mere acquaintances."

"Motive is only relevant when there's been a crime, Lady Rossex," Rivers replied as if he was reading from a policing manual. "As I keep saying, this could still turn out to be an accident."

Why is Rivers the only one still holding on to that theory?

Perry scoffed at the suggestion, rolling his eyes. "Oh, come on! Surely there are way too many coincidences for it to be an accident?"

"Coincidences happen, Mr Juke," Rivers replied coolly, his eyes narrowing.

Bea bit her lip, feeling a flare of frustration at Rivers' dismissiveness. *Fitzwilliam doesn't think so!*

Rivers continued, "It doesn't mean there's foul play involved. And in any case, I'll conduct my investigation as I see fit."

The room buzzed with angry murmurs, the tension between Rivers and the rest of them palpable. Bea's mind raced, searching for some way to convince Rivers of the urgency of the situation. They were close – so very close – to uncovering the truth, but without his cooperation, it felt like they were further away than ever.

Meed cleared his throat and stepped forward. "Sir," he said, his deep voice commanding attention. "Perhaps we could talk to Miss Parks about the jewel and see if it's hers."

Rivers regarded Meed for a moment, his expression unreadable. A heavy, suffocating silence filled the air. Bea held her breath, waiting for his response.

"Alright," Rivers conceded, sighing loudly. "We'll go and see what she has to say about it." He rose, then paused, facing Em. "In the meantime, I want you and your friends here to keep your noses out of this investigation from now on. Do I make myself clear?"

Em stood, her hands clasped tightly together. "Crystal."

"Good," Rivers mumbled, then turning to follow Meed, he stormed out of the room.

"Can you believe that man?" Perry waved his arms towards the door. "The nerve of him! Dismissing everything we've found so far like that."

There were murmurs of agreement from the rest of the room as Perry made his way the end of the table to join the others. Bea didn't move. Confusion weighed heavily on her mind. The evidence was mounting against Mel, but deep down, she was finding it difficult to imagine her as a cold-blooded killer who would've risked losing all she had to avenge the death of an ex-boyfriend who'd left her for someone else.

"Hey." Perry's voice broke through her thoughts. "How about we go to the bar for a drink? I know I could do with one."

"Great idea. I'd like to get out of this room," Claire said, already shuffling towards the door.

Ellie tipped her head. "Me too."

"Bea?" Em asked as she rose and made to follow the others.

A sudden throb in her head made Bea raise her hands and rub her temples. "I'll be there in a minute. I'm just going to pop up to my room and take a couple of headache tablets."

Em nodded. "Okay. We'll see you in a bit."

Alone in the quiet room, Bea let out a heavy sigh. *This is all such a mess.* Her headache intensified, her temples pulsing in time with her heartbeat. *I hope Rivers and Meed get some answers soon.* She didn't know how much more of this she could take.

28

FIVE MINUTES LATER, SATURDAY 13 MARCH

Walking down the plush corridor of the first floor of Chasingham House, Bea relished the brief respite from the others as she made her way to her room. She needed time to think. The soft glow from the antique sconces cast warm light onto the intricately patterned carpet that felt luxurious under-foot. A sudden flicker of movement at the far end of the corridor caught her eye. Squinting into the dim light, she made out the statuesque figure of a woman slipping down the staff staircase, clutching an overnight bag tightly to her chest. Something about the furtive motion of the woman piqued her curiosity, and her heart quickened with excitement. *Who on earth is that skulking around the hotel at this time of the evening?* Tucking an errant strand of her long, thick red hair behind her ear, she sped up, her sandals making barely a sound on the thick carpet.

As Bea drew closer to the staircase, she caught a glimpse of the red soles of a pair of high-heeled black leopard-print pumps that seemed oddly familiar. Then it hit her. The elegant shoes were the same ones Mel had been wearing on Friday when they'd all arrived at Chasingham House. She remembered admiring how elegantly Mel had managed to walk in the Louboutins with their towering heels. Bea had a pair, and she wobbled around in them like Bambi on ice, constantly worried she would roll her ankles.

Where's Mel going? Rivers and Meed couldn't have finished interviewing her already; they had only left ten minutes ago. *Oh, no!* The overnight bag. Using the staff staircase. *What if she's making a run for it?* She had to stop her!

As the plush carpet gave way to cold, uncarpeted stone steps that spiralled down into darkness, Bea cautiously followed the echoing footsteps below.

———

DS Meed scanned the hotel suite before him. The scent of expensive perfume lingered in the air, but there was no sign of Mel Parks.

"Well, where is she?" DCI Rivers barked at the impeccably dressed lawyer, his tailored suit crisp and his tie perfectly knotted, who was standing in the middle of the room.

The man cleared his throat. "I'm afraid I don't know where Miss Parks is at the moment. She was here just a few minutes ago." He looked around the room, his composed expression failing to hide a hint of worry.

Either he's a very good actor, or he's genuinely bewildered by her disappearance, Meed thought.

"Was she now?" Rivers did nothing to hide his scepticism.

The lawyer displayed a slight twitch in his left eye, and there were tiny beads of sweat forming on his brow. *He's worried.*

"Chief inspector, I assure you, I am telling the truth. I went to the bathroom, then I heard a knock on the door. I thought Mel would open it, but when you continued to knock so earnestly, I came out of the bathroom to find her gone," the lawyer insisted, his hands clasped tightly together as if trying to hold on to his composure. "Could she have gone to the bar maybe?"

Without hesitating, Meed's fingers quickly tapped out a message to Emma McKeer-Adler:

Vic Meed: *Have you seen Mel Parks? She's not in her suite. She could be in the bar maybe?*

Meed was pretty sure the DCI and her friends would have gone to the bar after he and Rivers had left them. He suppressed a sigh. What he would do for a cold beer right now…

The lawyer, a tall man with impeccably groomed hair, shifted his weight nervously from one foot to the other, clearly uncomfortable under Rivers' silent scrutiny. "I assure you, I have no idea where Miss Parks has gone."

"Really?" Rivers said, his voice cold and sharp. "Because if you don't help us find her, we'll have no choice but to track her down and arrest her ourselves." He gave the man a sly half-smile.

"Arrest her?" The lawyer's eyes widened in shock, then narrowed, a glint of challenge shining through as he crossed his arms over his chest. "You don't have any grounds to arrest Miss Parks," he stated firmly, squaring up to Rivers.

Oh no, he won't like that…

"Let's just say new information has come to light, and

your client is now a person of interest," Rivers replied, meeting the lawyer's gaze without flinching.

What a turnaround. Ten minutes ago, Rivers had been arguing that Mel Parks had no case to answer as it was all an accident, and now he was threatening to arrest her. *He's enjoying this*, Meed thought.

———

Perry tapped his newly-manicured fingers on the polished oak bar top, his ice-blue eyes scanning the room for any sign of Bea. The gentle hum of conversation filled the hotel's bar, punctuated by the occasional burst of laughter from Claire, Ellie, and the remaining birthday girls gathered in the corner. *Where is she?* She should have been down here by now. He turned his phone over. The screen was black. No message. *Is she unwell? Has something happened?* "Do you think I should go and see where Bea is?" he asked Em, who was perched next to him on a barstool.

"Well, I expect—" Her phone vibrated on the table in front of her. "Maybe that's her," she said, turning her phone over.

"Well?" Perry asked anxiously.

Em shook her head as she quickly typed out a response. "It's Meed. Mel isn't in her room. He's asking if she's down here in the bar with us."

Perry's heart thumped in time with his drumming fingers. "I don't like this, Em. Maybe she knows we're onto her…" If Mel was the murderer, as they suspected, then perhaps she'd discovered their suspicions and decided to flee. *Or worse…*

"Why don't we have a look around downstairs and see if we can find her?" Em said in hushed tones. She looked over at the group in the corner. "Let's not bother the others; they seem to be having a good time."

"What about Bea?"

"Don't worry," Em reassured him, placing her hand on his arm. "She's probably just having a lie down while her headache clears."

I hope so. He picked up his phone. *Shall I just call her?* He hesitated. He didn't want to wake her if she was napping. He opened up the text app.

Perry: *Are you okay? How's the headache? xx*

With a weary sigh, he scooted off the barstool, took a quick swig of his espresso martini, and followed Em out of the bar.

———

DS Vic Meed's phone buzzed in his hand.

DCI Emma McK-A: *No sign of Mel in the bar. I'll keep an eye out.*

"She's not in the bar, sir,"

"Well, my friend." Rivers turned to the lawyer. "You'd better hope you find your client before we do, or the next time you see her, you'll be visiting her at the station lockup."

"Fine," the lawyer replied, his voice tinged with frustration. "But I assure you, Miss Parks will have a lot to say about this."

"Let her," Rivers shot back, shrugging. "Right now, we just need to find her."

The lawyer let out a reluctant sigh. "Very well," he said, picking up his phone. "I'll do my best to locate her."

"See that you do," Rivers warned as he turned towards the door. "You know where to find me."

Meed suppressed a grin as he followed Rivers out. His boss might be an arrogant so-and-so most of the time, but he knew how to handle the likes of Mel's lawyer.

———

Bea crept cautiously down the staff staircase, her heart pounding in her chest. The faint scent of cleaning products hung in the air as she followed the *tap, tap* of Mel's shoes descending below. She came to the ground floor where a sign labelled 'reception' gleamed under the dim light, but the stairs continued to descend and so did the *tap, tap*.

Suddenly the sound stopped. Bea froze. Had Mel realised she was being followed? Was she waiting for her around the next corner? She held her breath. Then she heard it. A soft *thud, thud*. Carpet! The stairs must have ended. She let her breath out in a rush, then hurried on. The staircase ended abruptly, giving way to an ominous narrow corridor carpeted in a dark synthetic nylon pile. As her eyes adjusted, she spotted Mel not too far ahead, just turning into a passage on the right. *Where's she going?*

Her heart pounding against her ribs, she quickly ducked into the shadows of an alcove, wanting to wait until Mel was out of sight before daring to follow. Her breaths came shallow and quick as she clenched her hands in an effort to calm herself. *What on earth are you doing, Bea? Mel could be a murderer.* Richard Fitzwilliam's face flashed before her eyes.

He was scowling at her. It was as if she could hear his voice. "Don't do anything reckless like confront a murderer on your own," he said. *Oh dear, I'm going to be in so much trouble when he finds out…*

Bea's phone vibrated in her hand, the pulsing sensation grabbing her attention. She glanced at the screen and smiled at Perry's message. She'd forgotten all about the headache that had sent her to her room in the first place. *Ah, that's so sweet of him to be concerned about me.* Then she looked around at her surroundings. Actually, he would be even more concerned if he could see where she was right now! She typed a swift response, her thumbs dancing across the screen as her eyes remained trained on the corridor where Mel had vanished moments before.

Bea: *I'm following Mel. Think she's making a run for it. I seem to be in the basement. Assume she's looking for a door that leads outside? xx*

As soon as she hit send, her finger slid up to silence her phone. The last thing she needed was to alert Mel to her presence with an ill-timed call from Perry. She stuffed the phone down the front of her dress and tucked it under her bra strap. She stepped into the corridor and rushed towards the end where Mel had disappeared. She needed to find out where Mel was going.

29

MEANWHILE, SATURDAY 13 MARCH

Perry grabbed the door handle, feeling the cool brass on his fingers as he opened the door to Chasingham House's Garden Room. He glanced around, his sharp blue eyes scanning the room for any sign of Mel. *Nope!* Another empty room.

There was movement behind him. "Any luck, Perry?" Em asked, her voice laced with concern.

"Nothing." Perry sighed, frowning. "She doesn't seem to be anywhere on the ground floor, and we know she hasn't left the building." Their first stop had been reception. The two staff there had confirmed they hadn't seen Mel, and no one had entered or left the property this evening. A uniformed policeman had been standing just in the porch outside the entrance. She couldn't have gone that way. "Do you think she's gone to the spa?"

Em looked at her watch and shook her head. "I think it closed at seven."

Perry started as his phone buzzed in his pocket. Excitement and apprehension mingled in his chest. *Maybe it's from Bea?* Snatching it up, he read the text.

"Oh my giddy aunt!" He stared at the screen as his stomach plummeted to the floor.

"What is it?" Em looked up into his face. "What's wrong?"

"It's from Bea. She's in the basement. And she's following Mel!"

"What?" Em cried, leaning in to read the message. Her eyes widened as she absorbed the information. "Why is she only telling us now? We've been running around like headless chickens up here while she's following a possible murderer. Alone."

"Maybe she just stumbled across her and decided to follow her," Perry offered weakly, knowing full well that Bea's impulsive actions often led to exactly this situation. How many times over the last twelve months had he found himself running, literally, to get to her before she got into even more trouble?

"Just stumbled?" Em scoffed, her hands on her hips. "She's put herself in danger, Perry. Mel could be a killer, and Bea is on her own!" She took a deep breath. "Right. First things first. If Mel is in the basement, then we have to assume she's looking for a way out of the building."

"Agreed." Perry nodded, relief washing over him at the thought of having a plan to follow. *I just hope it doesn't involve running.* "She probably knows where she's going. Her father owns this place, remember."

"Let's find Greenhill. He'll know if there's a basement exit."

Perry hesitated. "Shouldn't we tell Rivers?"

"Yes, I suppose so. I'll text Meed," Em agreed reluctantly. She flipped over her phone, her fingers flying across the screen. "Right, that's done. Now let's go." She began to run back towards reception.

Perry cursed under his breath. *I knew we would end up running!*

———

Meed could feel the hum of the lift rattling through his body as it descended, the flickering overhead light casting shadows on the walls. His boss, Detective Chief Inspector Rivers, stood beside him, his arms crossed and his foot tapping impatiently as they made their way down to the ground floor to begin their search for Mel Parks. *Beep.* Rivers looked at him expectantly as he whipped his phone out of his jacket pocket and scanned the message from Emma McKeer-Adler.

"They've found her, sir. She's in the basement, presumably trying to get out of the building." He read the next section and stopped. *Oh no, Lady Beatrice is following her. Rivers will go mad!*

"Basement? What's going on? Who's that message from?" Rivers demanded, an edge to his voice.

Meed swallowed as he glanced at the floor number displayed on the lift's internal screen. They were almost at the ground floor. *That won't give Rivers time to totally kill me.* "Er, it's from DCI McKeer-Adler. Apparently, Lady Beatrice is following Miss Parks." He hunched his shoulders and turned his face away, waiting for the explosion.

"I specifically told them to keep their noses out of this investigation!" Rivers bellowed, his voice echoing in the confines of the lift.

Meed turned to his boss, whose face was now a violent shade of purple, his nostrils flared like an enraged bull. "Well, sir," he said cautiously, "I did ask the DCI if Miss Parks was in the bar."

"It was a simple question, Meed. It required a yes or no

reply. It didn't involve any action!" Rivers snapped, jabbing a finger at him for emphasis. "And of all people, a member of the royal family is now running after a murderer!"

Possible murderer. Meed hesitated. Best not to correct him right now though. But he did agree with his boss. Despite her royal status, Lady Beatrice seemed to have little regard for protocol or authority. *Are all the royal family like this?* He refocussed his mind. "Should we head to the basement now and see if we can find them?" he suggested, hoping to steer the conversation away from Lady Beatrice's involvement.

Rivers pursed his lips, then stabbed at the button with a large B on it. "Fine. Let's just hope Lady Beatrice knows what she's doing."

———

I've no idea what I'm doing. The damp, musty air clung to Bea's nostrils as she peered slowly around the corner of the corridor Mel had turned into a minute ago. Her pulse quickened at the sight of a door being opened at the end of the passageway. *Click.* Light from outside blasted in, casting an ethereal glow on Mel's statuesque form as she moved through the doorway. Bea's heart raced; she couldn't let Mel lock the door and disappear again.

She sprinted towards the door, her heart pounding in time with her footsteps. The door was almost closed when Bea reached it, but with a burst of adrenaline-fuelled strength, she threw her hand forward, stopping it from shutting. The sound of Mel swearing filled her ears. Then the woman forcefully pushed against the door. Bea leaned her shoulder against the wood and pushed back hard.

"Leave me alone!" Mel cried, her finishing school tones shining through.

"No!" Bea retorted, pushing back with all her might. "What are you doing, Mel? The police are everywhere. You won't get away." She hoped she was right. But what if the uniform police officer stationed outside had left?

"Lady Beatrice?" The pressure on the door subsided briefly, and gathering all her strength, Bea heaved against it with every ounce of energy she had left. The door groaned under the pressure, and a surprised yelp came from the other side as Mel lost her footing and crashed to the ground.

Bea lunged forward, propelling herself through the doorway just as Mel scrambled back up to her feet. Their eyes locked. Mel's flashing blue eyes were illuminated by the harsh glare of the security light outside.

———

Perry, his face flushed and his chest heaving, burst into the lobby of Chasingham House. His well-styled blond hair was now damp with sweat, and he could feel the pinch of his trendy boots as they squashed his little toes painfully into the expensive Italian leather. *I'm not made to run!*

"Mr Greenhill!" Em, already ahead of him, had opened the door to the right of the reception desk and was shouting into it, her voice echoing around the lavish hotel lobby.

A young female receptionist jumped up from behind the desk, clearly startled by the sudden commotion. "Can I help you?" she asked, her eyes darting between Perry and Em as though trying to gauge the urgency of the situation.

"Where's Mr Greenhill?" Em demanded, leaning in over the polished wooden desk, her short legs dangling just off the floor. She scanned behind the counter as if she expected to see him crouched down there hiding from her. "I need to speak to him immediately!"

"Er, he's probably making his rounds of the hotel," the receptionist replied nervously, her fingers fidgeting with a pen. "Would you like me to leave a message?"

Perry brushed away a bead of sweat dripping down his temple and rushed over to join Em.

"No, I don't want to leave a message," Em replied, her voice laced with frustration.

Perry spotted a two-way radio like the ones they had at Francis Court resting next to the receptionist. He pointed to it. "Can you get hold of him on that?" he asked, gasping for breath as he pointed towards the radio. "It's urgent."

The receptionist's fingers trembled as she fumbled with the radio, inadvertently filling the room with a cacophony of static and feedback. Perry winced at the sound, his ears ringing from its intensity.

"Mr Greenhill?" the woman stammered into the radio, her voice barely audible over the din of the device. "Are you there? We have er…a…situation at the front desk."

There was a brief pause punctuated by the crackle of the radio's speaker before Mr Greenhill's deep, authoritative voice came through. "Yes, I'm here," he replied, the calm in his tone a stark contrast to the urgency gripping Perry. "What's the problem?"

Without waiting for the receptionist to reply, Em lunged forward and snatched the radio from her grasp. "Mr Greenhill," she barked into the handset, her voice firm and unwavering. "This is DCI McKeer-Adler. We need to know where the exit from the basement comes out. It's a matter of life and death!"

———

The lift came to a sudden stop, and the doors slid open with a faint creak. Meed hurried out, his eyes darting around the shadowy basement.

"Down there?" Rivers whispered from beside him.

A narrow corridor stretching out before them. "Looks like it," Meed muttered, swallowing hard as he stared down the hallway.

"Right then, let's get moving," Rivers said, taking the lead.

As they hurried down the dimly lit corridor, Meed's heart thumped in his chest, echoing the rhythm of their footsteps. *Please let us get there on time. I don't want another person dead. Especially not a member of the royal family!*

30

AT THE SAME TIME, SATURDAY 13 MARCH

Bea's heart stilled as she and Mel stared at each other, tension thrumming between them like a taut violin string. *If she runs, am I going to risk taking a dive at her?*

"Lady Beatrice, what are you doing here?" Mel asked, her voice barely above a whisper.

"I saw you going down the stairs as I was on my way to my room," Bea replied, trying to sound casual despite the adrenaline coursing through her veins. "I know the police want to talk to you, so I followed you to see where you're going." Her gaze drifted downwards, landing on the overnight bag that lay abandoned on the ground by Mel's feet. "Were you planning on running away?" she asked, unable to keep the suspicion from seeping into her voice.

Mel clenched her jaw, then glanced away.

Will she lie to me?

"Yes...I was," she said, a tremor in her voice.

She looks so vulnerable. Mel let out a shuddering breath, and her hands went limp by her sides. This was nothing like the confident Mel that Bea was used to. *But then it could all just be an act to make me feel sorry for her.*

"Where were you going to go?" Bea asked gently.

"My father has a private jet at an airport in Surrey. I thought…" Her voice trailed off to barely a whisper.

"Mel, running away won't solve anything," Bea said softly. "The police won't just give up. They won't let a murderer hide from them for long."

Mel looked away, her breaths coming in shaky gasps. "But I'm not a murderer," she choked out. "At least…I mean…I never expected Mercy to die. That's not what I wanted."

Bea frowned. Mel knew Mercy had had a serious allergy to mango. What did she think she'd needed the EpiPen for? "What do you mean? What did you want to happen?"

"I…I just wanted her to be ill," Mel stammered, her hands trembling at her sides. "Maybe get a nasty rash. That's what I heard happens to people with allergies. I didn't know she would die because of it!"

"But you took her EpiPen so she couldn't help herself," Bea said, her voice thick with emotion. She hated seeing Mel crumble before her eyes like this. She wanted to believe what she was saying, but—

"No, I didn't!" Mel cried, her eyes widening with what looked like genuine surprise. "I didn't even know she had one."

Bea frowned, her mind racing with possibilities. Had someone else taken the pen? Or was Mel lying? Yet, seeing the normally calm and slightly aloof Mel in such a state, Bea found it difficult to believe she was making it all up.

"Alright," Bea said, rubbing her hands together, trying to create a little warmth in the chilly night air. "Why don't you tell me what happened? Start from the beginning."

Mel hesitated for a moment, then let out a shaky breath. "I knew of her, of course — Mercy, Vikki's American friend from New York, but I'd never met her before this weekend. Vikki had said on the WhatsApp group that her mother had put her under pressure to invite Mercy along—" She stopped. "Sorry, that doesn't matter." She took another gulp of air and carried on, "Anyway, it started ten years ago. I was working in New York and was having coffee with someone I'd met at the gym; she was called Cass. This handsome guy came over and said hi. Ross worked with her. They were both lawyers. He got my number from Cass and asked me if we could go out for a coffee. He told me he had a clingy girlfriend called Sadie, but he wasn't in love with her."

Sadie? Ah, as in Mercedes…

"When we realised we were attracted to each other, he said he would end it. He was so good like that. He always wanted to do the right thing. Later, he said she'd taken it badly, and his parents and hers, who were very close friends, had given him a hard time. He said they would all come around eventually. In the meantime we would concentrate on just us. It was blissful. New York in the fall. Just the two of us. We were so in love. Two months of sightseeing, theatre visits, romantic weekends out of town. I really thought I'd died and gone to Heaven." As Mel spoke, her eyes grew distant, lost in the memories of a time now tainted by tragedy. "Then suddenly it was all ripped away from me."

She looked over at Bea, her eyes shimmering with unshed tears. "I'll never forget the look on Ross' face when he walked into the flat on that fateful evening. Even though he had his own apartment on the other side of town, since we'd got together, he'd been staying with me near Central Park. He'd looked like someone had stripped him of all feeling, like he was a zombie. He'd come back from dinner with his parents. He'd wanted to take me too, but they'd said it was too soon." There was a hitch in her voice. She paused to swipe at a tear that had rolled down her cheek.

"He dropped onto the sofa and put his head in his hands. I ran over and asked him what was wrong. He looked up at me, still in a trance, and shook his head. I knew it was serious. I grabbed him a drink. He took it with shaking hands. Slowly, he told me what had happened. He'd turned up at his parents only to find Sadie and her parents were there too. He was furious and threatened to leave, but they told him he had to stay and listen. Then they told him Sadie was twelve weeks pregnant. She'd just found out that morning, and she'd told her parents immediately. They in turn had rung Ross' parents. They had all agreed they needed to discuss it as a 'family'. I was frantic. I asked him if he was sure he was the father. But he shook his head sadly and told me Sadie was many things, but she wouldn't have cheated on him. We were both in tears. Then he dropped the *real* bombshell." Mel stopped and took in a shaky, shallow breath.

Something tickled Bea's face. She reached up and was surprised to feel her cheek was wet. *Get a grip, Bea! She might be making this all up just to get your sympathy so you'll let her go.*

"They were to get married in two weeks' time. Both sets of parents insisted so it would be before Sadie began to show. I protested. I told him that they couldn't make him marry her, but he shook his head. I could see he was defeated already. He told me he was sorry, but he had to do the right thing."

Tears were now streaming down Mel's face. She slowly shook her head. "I told him he had no backbone. He just kept saying sorry. I shouted at him to leave. He left. I was devastated."

She wiped her coat sleeve across her face. *She looks just as devastated now*, Bea thought, squashing her instinct to reach out and envelop Mel in a hug. *No one is that good of an actress. This part of the story must be true.*

Mel sniffed loudly, then took a ragged breath in before letting it out slowly while she seemed to get a hold of herself. "I stayed in New York for those two weeks, pitifully hoping Ross would see sense and back out. I sent him messages begging him to reconsider. He patiently replied that he had to do the right thing. I carried on. I told him my life was over. He said sorry. Then he blocked me. I tried to find out where the wedding was. I wanted to go and see for myself. I wanted to shout out that he was mine. But his friends stopped taking my calls." She shrugged sadly. "I saw the article in the society page of the *New York Times*. Ross Coles, lawyer and Harvard graduate, son of New York district attorney Harold Coles, and society hostess Andrea Coles, married Sadie Bushy, daughter of US Diplomat Richard Bushy, and his wife, the novelist Claire Bright. It was a small celebration for family and close friends at a prestigious venue in the Hamptons. There were no pictures. I cried for twenty-four hours. Then I called my father and told him I wanted to come home."

Bea rubbed her arms. *I wish I had a coat.* Mel was looking down at the grass. She gave a heavy sigh as she looked up at Bea with red puffy eyes. "It may sound crazy, but even after the wedding, I thought maybe Ross and I would still be together one day. A marriage couldn't work in those circumstances, could it? So I thought one day, he would realise it, and so….I would wait for him."

Her chin trembled, then she continued, "Two months after I got home, I was woken by a call during the night. It was from the woman I met over there — Cass. She said she was so sorry, but she had bad news. Ross had been found in the East River. They didn't know what had happened exactly, but he'd left a note in his office addressed to his parents. For days I couldn't believe it. I scoured the New York papers. Then three days later, a small article confirmed that Ross Coles had died. There were no details, just a comment that the police weren't treating it as a suspicious death. Two weeks later there was a write-up of the funeral. And a picture of his widow. She was young, with long dark hair and holding a hankie to her mouth. She didn't look pregnant. I called Cass and asked her if Sadie was pregnant. She was reluctant to say anything at first, but eventually she told me that yes, at first Ross had told her that Sadie was pregnant, but then nothing more was said. But shortly after, she'd noticed he wasn't eating much and seemed really unhappy, so she'd asked him what was wrong. He'd said they'd lost the baby at sixteen weeks. He'd said Sadie was a mess, but he didn't know how to feel about it."

Mel took in a big gulp of air. "Then Cass told me something really shocking. She said a few weeks later, she'd found Ross late one evening in his office with his head in his hands. He'd told her he now believed Sadie had never been pregnant. He'd thought the whole thing had been a rouse cooked up by her and her parents to get him to marry her. He'd even thought that maybe his own parents knew too. He'd said he couldn't trust anyone anymore." Mel swallowed, then shook her head. "That was two days before he died."

Bea groaned. "Oh, Mel. I'm so sorry."

They stood in silence for a few minutes, then Mel cleared her throat. "So imagine my shock when Sadie, now calling herself Mercy, turned up at Chasingham House. Of course, I didn't know it was her at first. We were all in the bar together having coffee, and I thought she looked a bit familiar, but that was all. Then we had some champagne, and everyone began to relax. We started talking about relationships. Flick was saying what a disaster her marriage was. Then Cammy was whining about how her useless boyfriend had cheated on her. We all laid into Cammy a bit as her ex is a womaniser and a bully. None of us like him. Vikki said men were no good, and we should all turn lesbian; it was so much easier."

She gave a wry smile. "I was saying I thought marriage was an old fashioned institution and to be avoided at all costs. That's my MO — I don't believe in marriage. I hide behind that all the time. Of course if Ross had asked me, I would have jumped at it. But now…no one else is good enough, but it's easier to blame the idea than explain that I'd lost the only man I ever wanted to marry." She sighed. "Then Flick asked Mercy what she thought. She was all weird about it. She looked embarrassed. She mumbled something about marriage shouldn't be the be all and end all, then she excused herself to go to the bathroom. After she left, Flick asked if she'd said something wrong. Vikki told us Mercy had been married in her mid-twenties, but he'd died within a few months of the wedding. She'd suggested maybe we'd hit a nerve. Flick, who is much more sensitive than the rest of us, then rushed off to the bathroom to find her and apologise. Even then I didn't make the connection. But then Flick came back and said Mercy had gone to her room to rest before lunch. She said they'd had a chat, and Mercy had explained that they believed her husband had taken his own life, and she still finds it hard to talk about. We were all sympathetic at that point."

Bea nodded. *Well, you would be, wouldn't you?*

"I was first down to lunch, and Mercy arrived shortly after me. I asked her if she was okay, and she apologised. She said she shouldn't drink so much. She said that it was ten years ago since Ross had died, so she should be able to talk about it by now. I could hardly respond. I thought it had to be a coincidence, didn't it? But I had to find out for sure, so I said that it must have been so hard for her and asked her what had happened.

"She said they'd only been married a few months when he died. She said they'd had a small wedding in the Hamptons. I remember I gasped and had to pretend my coffee was too hot. Then she said her husband Ross had been found in the East River by two late-night fisherman. She'd thought he had been working late. I asked if it was an accident. She said he'd left a letter in his office for his parents. She never saw it, but the police said it suggested he'd taken his own life. The autopsy confirmed he'd taken an overdose of Tylenol and then CCTV followed him to the river where he disappeared."

Mel took a deep breath, her eyes shining with tears. "I was trying so hard not to cry. My poor Ross. So she was Sadie. I made the right sympathetic noises and then asked her where the name Mercy came from. She explained her name is really Mercedes, but she hated having the same name as a car — too many ride jokes. She told me she used to be called Sadie when she was younger, but she preferred Mercy now." Mel shook her head. "The woman who took my Ross away from me was sitting right next to me. I felt sick to my stomach. I blamed the champagne and left. When I got to my room, I threw up."

Mel lifted her chin, giving Bea a defiant look. "It was then I decided I wanted to hurt her for what she'd done to me and Ross."

31

MEANWHILE OVER HERE,
SATURDAY 13 MARCH

Perry's heart pounded in his chest as he sprinted through the darkness, guided only by the feeble light of his smartphone. The cold night air whipped at his face, stinging his eyes. He adjusted his grip on his phone. Beside him, Em puffed loudly, her breath visible in the chilly night air.

His boots were pinching his feet with every step. *Why do I always end up running in unsuitable shoes?* Not that there was anything Perry *really* considered suitable to run in. He preferred not to run at all.

"This way," Em shouted as she ran around the southwest corner of the house. "Greenhill said...the tradesman's entrance...to the basement...is on the northwest corner... It can't be far away..." she said between breaths.

He followed her around the side of the house, trying to ignore the pain in his feet. He knew all too well the kind of danger Bea could be in if she confronted Mel alone. She'd been in this position before. And although her self-defence skills were pretty impressive, having attended a kidnapping prevention course a few years ago, Mel could have a weapon.

His heart dropped in his chest. *Please be careful, Bea. I need you by my side at my wedding.*

———

Meed's pulse surged as he moved through the dimly lit basement corridor alongside Rivers. The damp, musty air clung to his skin like a second layer of clothing as they hurried along, the lights from their phones flickering against the peeling wallpaper and cobwebs adorning the passage. He slowed down as he turned the corner. *A light!* He turned to whisper to Rivers, who had fallen behind him a little. "I can see what looks like a partly open door, sir." A shard of light spilled into the passage, and a flicker of hope ignited within him.

He stopped as faint voices wafted through the air. He strained to listen, his mouth going dry as he recognised the plummy tones of Lady Beatrice and Mel Parks. He closed his eyes for a moment. *Thank goodness they're both still alive.* Rivers caught him up. He turned. "I can hear them." Meed's voice was hushed but urgent. "It sounds like Lady Beatrice and Mel Parks."

Rivers nodded as he caught his breath. "Right. We need to approach this carefully, sergeant. We don't want to alert them to our presence," he whispered.

Meed gave him a thumbs up as he crept towards the lit doorway.

———

Bea shivered as the cold penetrated her bones. She didn't want to stop Mel talking. She was clearly upset but still seemed quite calm and reasonable. Bea knew from previous encounters with killers that it could turn at any moment. And even though Mel didn't look like a threat to her right now as she stood wiping the tears from her cheeks, the wrong word or a unexpected movement, and suddenly her life could be in danger. She loosened up her shoulders. She needed to be ready in case it got physical. "So what happened, Mel?"

"I know Daddy has a big bottle of potassium chloride in his suite; he has hypokalaemia and takes a diluted amount each day, so he keeps a bottle here. I also know if you get the dose wrong, then it gives you a really bloated stomach and makes you sick. I thought if I added some to a cocktail and gave it to her, she'd have a bad night."

Ah, so that explains the missing potassium chloride!

"But in the end I didn't use it," she said in a shaky voice. "I wish I had now, Bea." Her eyes filled with tears again. "Then she would still be alive!" The tears spilled down her face.

Bea resisted the urge to step forward and comfort her. *She could still be a murderer! Models have to be actors as well. This could all be fake...* "So what made you change your mind?"

She sniffed and let out a ragged breath.

"I knew Daddy said he can taste it even diluted in water. So I thought I'd talk to Jarvis, the bartender, to try and find out which cocktail had the strongest taste. After my treatment, I went to the bar. And who should be in there but Mercy. She was nursing a glass of champagne. Jarvis was nowhere to be seen, so I sat down next to her, and I was looking at the special cocktail menu that had been put out everywhere. She said she was looking forward to the cocktails later. I thought it would be the perfect time to find out what cocktail she preferred. So I told her I fancied the magnificent mango moucher and asked her which one she liked the look of. She said she was sure it would be delightful, but she couldn't have one as she had an allergy to mangos."

Mel paused and sniffed again, then looking down at the ground, she slowly shook her head. "I thought I'd stumbled onto a much better plan. She said it would give her a rash, and I thought that was better. It would be more obvious, and maybe the symptoms would last longer than the potassium chloride. And itch. I really wanted it to itch." She dragged her hand through her short swept-back hair. She looked at Bea with pleading eyes. "Is this karma? I wanted to make her suffer more, and this is my punishment, knowing that I killed her?"

What could she say? Bea still wasn't totally sure Mel hadn't known exactly what she'd been doing. "What happened that evening?" Bea asked in a soothing tone.

"I ordered the mango cocktail and just waited for my chance to put some in Mercy's drink," Mel replied, staring out into the darkness. "It wasn't that easy. She never seemed to put her glass down. I was almost ready to give up when Vikki asked me to help get Mercy up to her room. When we got her upstairs, she was still pretty drunk, but she said she was okay, so we left her. I followed Vikki out and as I went past the table, I swiped Mercy's spare room keycard. I went back down. I waited fifteen minutes, then I told everyone I had to attend a webinar. I took my mango cocktail and went up to my room."

She took a deep breath, then looked up and caught Bea's eyes. "You might not believe me, but as I started to watch the webinar, I got cold feet. I asked myself what was the point. Then someone in the webinar asked a question, and their name scrolled up. They were called Ross." She balled her fists. "And it hurt so much. Just seeing his name. It was enough to make me stick with the plan."

Her posture crumpled, and she released her hands, wiggling her fingers by her sides. "I went to her room and knocked on her door. When she didn't reply, I let myself in. She was over in a chair by the window, dozing. She still had a half-full strawberry cocktail on the table in front of her, so I emptied most of mine into her glass. Then I gently shook her awake. She was still a little drunk and took a while to come around. I told her I'd come to check up on her. I asked her if she was okay and if I could help her. She sobered up a bit, so I sat down and encouraged her to talk. I asked her where she'd lived in America, and she started to babble on about New York City and how vibrant it was. I told her to drink up, and I took a sip of what was left of my drink too. I really wasn't sure she would just drink it like she did. She practically necked the whole thing in one go. Then I told her to get some rest. I dropped her key back on the table as I left."

"And did you take her EpiPen and allergy card?"

"No." Mel frowned. "Did she have one?" She blinked rapidly. "But why didn't she use it?"

Bea stared at the woman before her. She seemed genuinely shocked. Could she have been telling the truth all along? Had she accidentally killed Mercy? *Poor Mel.* Bea's chest tightened. *I believe her.* Maybe Mercy had never had the EpiPen and card on her after all?

Suddenly over Mel's shoulder, she saw two flickering lights heading towards them. *Is someone out there?* She narrowed her eyes to try to figure out what she was looking at. Then she jumped out of her skin as Mel reached out and grabbed her arm.

———

Oh no! A wave of nausea hit Perry as Mel grabbed his best friend. *She's going to kill Bea!* He gritted his teeth and dug deeper. He sped up. *Don't worry, Bea. We're almost there...*

———

Has Mel Parks got to the end of her story? Meed looked down at his phone. The red record light was still flashing. He couldn't believe he'd managed to get her admission that she'd given Mercy the mango on purpose. *She's just admitted to murder! Wait!* She'd said she hadn't taken the EpiPen and allergy card. *Was she telling the truth or—*

"What's happening?" Rivers hissed into his ear.

Meed frowned. It had gone quiet. Too quiet...

32

JUST THEN, SATURDAY 13 MARCH

Bea's heart pounded in her chest as Mel's long manicured fingers wrapped around her arm with an iron grip. The security light above the basement exit cast an eerie glow on Mel's face, making her ice-blue eyes seem even more piercing. "Ouch! Mel, get off!" Bea's voice wavered slightly despite her best efforts to remain calm. The model loosened her grip.

"I'm sorry, but I promise I didn't mean to do it, Lady Beatrice. I swear! You have to believe me," she said, her eyes pleading with Bea. "I never wanted her dead. I just—"

Suddenly Perry, his blond hair glistening under the security light, came barrelling towards them, followed closely by Em who cried out, "Police! Let go of Lady Beatrice now, Mel!" Bea's heart leaped at the sight of her friends. Would they agree with her that Mel hadn't meant to kill Mercy? That she wasn't a cold-blooded killer?

"Bea!" Perry's shout pierced through the night as he and Em charged towards Mel. Bea tugged her arm free. *Oh no!* Did they think Mel was attacking her? "Wait!" she screamed just as a hand clamped onto her shoulder from behind. *What the—* Bea's reflexes kicked in. Her heart racing, adrenaline flooding her system, she swung around, and her fist connected with her assailant's face. A sharp cry of pain filled the air followed by a *thump* as someone hit the ground.

Beside her, Perry and Em threw themselves at Mel, who was still standing, attempting to subdue her. Mel fought back, her statuesque frame thrashing wildly in an effort to break free from their grasps.

What on earth is going on?

"Melanie Parks!" a commanding voice bellowed over the cacophony. "You're under arrest for the murder of Mercy Bright!"

Rivers? Her heart sank. She hardly dared to look behind her. Gingerly, she swivelled around. *Rats!* Meed was scrambling to his feet, his nose dripping with blood.

"DS Meed?" Bea stammered, staring at the detective with wide eyes. "I...I'm so sorry!"

The man shrugged, getting a handkerchief from his pocket and holding it up to his face. "Isokay," he mumbled as he dabbed it carefully under his nose.

"I didn't mean to kill her!" Mel protested as Perry and Em held on to an arm each.

"You can let her go now, Ms Adler, Mr Juke," Rivers barked at full volume. "I can take it from here."

"Miss Parks!" A new voiced entered the fray. Mel's lawyer ran towards them, his arm outstretched. "Don't say anything else, Miss Parks." The tall man turned to Rivers, who was dangling a pair of handcuffs in one hand while attempting to wrestle his client from Em's grasp with the other. "Let her go, Rivers!"

In the midst of the confusion, DS Meed's phone rang, cutting through the chaos like a knife. Em and Rivers ceased playing tug of war with Mel, and Rivers quickly clamped the cuffs on her before her lawyer could get any closer.

Perry ran over to Bea and grabbed her hand as Meed moved away from the group to take the call.

Bea's head swam. She opened her mouth to speak, but nothing came out. She was completely speechless. Perry squeezed her fingers and whispered in her ear. "I think Meed will have a black eye tomorrow."

33

11 PM, SATURDAY 13 MARCH

The dim lighting of Space flickered off the polished glassware as Bea huddled together with her friends. Their party was the only one still in the bar, and the low hum of their conversation echoed against the walls, creating an intimate atmosphere. Bea, Perry, and Em had just finished filling Claire and Ellie in on the evening's events. The two women listened with rapt attention, their faces a mixture of shock and disbelief.

"Blimey," Ellie muttered, shaking her head and running a hand through her long wispy light-brown hair. "I'm still trying to wrap my head around all of this."

"Same here," Claire agreed, adjusting her glasses with one hand while absently stirring her drink with the other. Her curly brown hair bounced as she nodded emphatically. "So you're saying you all thought Mel was attacking Bea, so you tried to stop her, and meanwhile you, Bea, thought you were being attacked by some unknown assailant, who was really DS Meed, and you punched him in the face."

Perry shifted his weight, his slightly muddy dinner suit

rustling with the movement. "And that's your takeaway from this, is it?" he asked, a sarcastic tinge to his voice.

Claire giggled. "Well, it's not very often a member of the royal family assaults a police officer."

Em smiled. "I would say never," she added.

Heat crept up Bea's neck. "Yes, thank you, everyone. I didn't know he was a pol—"

"Bea, we're teasing!" Em jumped in. "Although remind me to never creep up on you!" She mimed being punched on the nose, and they all laughed.

Bea suddenly wished Fitzwilliam was here with them; she'd like to tell him all about what had happened and hear his view on Mel's guilt. But then, what would he say when he found out she'd followed Mel this evening? Would he point out that she'd been headstrong and put herself in danger just like she'd done in the past? *Will he be disappointed that I got into a scrape again?*

"Bea," Claire began hesitantly, drawing Bea out of her thoughts of Fitzwilliam. "Do you really believe Mel didn't know that the mango would kill Mercy?"

Bea took a sip of her espresso martini, the bittersweet concoction perking her up and soothing her at the same time. "Indeed, I do," she replied, her voice firm. "But I can't make sense of what happened to the EpiPen and allergy card."

Em leaned forward, her eyebrows raised. "Well, when the police search Mel's bags and room, they might turn up. If they do, then we'll all know she was lying."

Perry pursed his lips, folding his arms across his chest. "That depends on whether her smarty-pants lawyer will let them search her stuff without a warrant, and that could take a while."

"Actually," Em replied, "because Mel is under arrest, the

police have the right to search her room and possessions without a warrant. So he won't be able to stop them."

Ellie, who had been quietly sipping her mojito, suddenly spoke up. "You know, I feel sorry for Mel. To lose the love of her life because his parents conspired with Mercy and her parents to trick him into marriage is despicable behaviour."

Claire peered at Ellie with raised eyebrows. "True, but we only have Mel's version of what happened. It's not like Mercy can dispute it now that she's dead."

Well, she does have a point.

Beep! Em grabbed her phone from the table in front of her. She studied the screen. "It's DS Meed asking where we are. He has an update for us." Her fingers tapped out a response.

As the conversation continued around her, Bea's thoughts turned to Mel. Had they taken her to the station, or was she still in the building, her lawyer fighting to stop them taking her to jail? She hoped they wouldn't find the pen and allergy card in Mel's possession. She really wanted to believe Mel had not intended to kill Mercy.

She slumped back in her seat; it was as if all her energy had been sucked out of her. A faint smile crossed her lips as she recalled Fitzwilliam's words after their first case together: "Once the burst of adrenaline wears off, it's normal to feel drained." How right he was.

"Bea?" Em came and crouched down beside her. "I thought I'd just let you know that I've had a word with Mr Greenhill about him offering Vikki prescription sleeping tablets. He's mortified. He said he was just trying to help her as she'd been with him when they'd discovered the body, and he knew how disturbing that had been for both of them. The sleeping tablets he offered her were his own, prescribed by his doctor a few months ago when he'd suffered from a bout of insomnia."

So he was just being kind and thoughtful. Her ears felt impossibly hot. *I'm such an idiot!* She sighed. It was Mrs Crammond all over again.

Em continued, "Anyway, Meed and I have discussed it, and we agree we don't need to take any further action. I think Greenhill was just trying to be helpful. It's unlikely that it's something he's ever done before, and I certainly don't think it's something he'll do again in a hurry." She placed her hand on Bea's arm. "But thank you for saying something. With all the celebrities and rich folk who come here, it would be the perfect place for someone to run a racket like that." She patted Bea's arm. "You would've made a good police officer, you know," she said, smiling.

Bea pulled herself forward in her chair and took in a deep breath. She lifted her chin as she smiled back. "Thanks, Em."

Just then the door to the bar creaked open, and as Bea's eyes flicked towards the entrance, the weary figure of Meed filled the doorway. His tie was slightly askew, and he looked like he'd been running on nothing but caffeine and determination for hours. Below a puffy eye, his nose was red and swollen.

Bea winced. *He looks how I feel!*

"I thought I'd come and give you an update," he said in nasally tones, a thin smile on his battered face.

Em straightened up. "Thanks, sergeant, it's much appreciated. Would you like a drink?"

"No thank you, ma'am. I've had enough coffee to keep the entire navy afloat. I doubt I'll sleep for a week." He sat down next to Em and placed his phone on the table. "So Mel has been de-arrested, then voluntarily questioned under caution at the station with her lawyer present. He wouldn't let her say much, and she's now been released."

"What does that mean?" Ellie asked.

Meed gave her a wry smile. "It means she's not been charged yet, although she might be in the—"

"Are you serious?" Perry interjected, his face a mixture of disbelief and concern. "But she could be a murderer!"

"That call I took when we first apprehended her was from Mrs Bright's mother," Meed explained, rubbing the back of his neck. "Their housekeeper found her EpiPen and allergy card in her London bedroom. Seems she didn't bring them with her. Her mother is devastated, as you can imagine."

"But I don't understand," Claire said, a frown creasing her forehead. "If Mercy knew she had a deadly allergy, why did she leave behind the one thing that could save her life?"

Meed shook his head. "Her mother said Mrs Bright had read somewhere that the reaction she'd had before, that had necessitated the trip to A&E, wouldn't necessarily occur again. She said her daughter could be very headstrong, and she didn't want to accept that she had a life-threatening condition."

Bea's heart twisted in her chest. So this could all have been prevented if only Mercy had taken her allergy seriously.

"Wait a minute," Perry said, his voice shaking slightly. "So that means Mel wasn't lying about not knowing the severity of Mercy's allergy. She didn't mean to kill her."

"From what she's told us, yes," Meed confirmed, his expression sombre. "She may still face a manslaughter charge, but her lawyer will likely argue she acted under duress, and that possible cross-contamination in the bar could have also contributed to Mrs Bright's death. Plus, the jewel they found in her room could have come from anywhere. I suspect he will try and agree a plea bargain of some sort."

Perry's face flushed with indignation. "So she'll just get away with it?" he fumed, his blue eyes flashing with anger. "That's outrageous!"

"Look, Perry," Ellie began, her voice calm and deliberate. "All Mel really did was try to give Mercy an embarrassing rash for a few days. She never meant to kill her. So why should she be punished like a cold-blooded murderer? Besides, Mercy didn't tell anyone about the allergy, so doesn't that make her partly culpable too?"

Claire chimed in, her red glasses sliding down her nose as she waved her arms at her friend. "But we can't ignore the fact someone died! Intent or not, Mel played a part in that."

While the three of them began a heated debate about moral responsibility and victim blaming, Em and Meed discussed possible charges that could be brought against Mel.

Bea sat quietly, sipping her espresso martini. *It's done now. It's not up to us anymore.* She sighed deeply as she sank into her chair, her limbs heavy and her mind somewhat foggy. This hadn't turned out to be the relaxing weekend they'd all hoped for, but as she glanced around at her friends, their faces animated and passionate, her heart swelled with joy. They were so lucky to have each other. Even if they didn't always agree!

A squeeze on her arm raised her from her sleepiness, and she smiled at Perry as he sat down next to her.

"You look like you're in another world," he said, gently nudging her.

"Sorry, I'm just tired," she said, nudging him back. "I'm sorry this didn't end up being the quiet, relaxing weekend you'd hoped for."

"Quiet and relaxing are overrated," he replied, grinning. "When I spoke to Simon last night, it was still raining in The Lakes, and so far, they've barely broken a sweat, let alone any bones. I bet, in the end, we'll have had a more adrenaline-fuelled weekend than them." He picked up his dry martini and raised it to her. "Thank you for an unexpectedly diverting weekend."

34

MORNING, SUNDAY 21 MARCH

The Society Page online article:

Members of the Royal Family Attend the Wedding of Crime Writer and Celebrity Chef Simon Lattimore to the Countess of Rossex's Business Partner Perry Juke

Yesterday Her Royal Highness Princess Helen (63), along with her husband Charles Astley (64), the Duke of Arnwall, their daughters Lady Beatrice (36), the Countess of Rossex, and Lady Sara Rosdale (39), and their son Lord Frederick Astley (39), were guests at the highly anticipated wedding of Perry Juke (34), Lady Beatrice's business partner, and Simon Lattimore (40), the celebrated crime novelist and past winner of Celebrity Elitechef.

The wedding took place in the Orangery at Francis Court, the sixteenth duke's ancestral home. Mr Lattimore looked ultra-smart in his cream tuxedo jacket and was accompanied by his best woman Roisin McNally, who looked elegant in a floral rose gown despite having her arm in a cast. Ms McNally had been injured on the last day of Mr Lattimore's bachelor party in the Lake District last weekend. Mr Juke, wearing a stylish morning suit, was attended by his best woman Lady Beatrice, who was dressed in a stunning silk cherry-print gown.

After the service, the seventy-five guests were treated to an exquisite eight-course tasting menu designed by Mr Lattimore, Lady Beatrice's son Samual Wilshire (14), and TV chef, Ryan Hawley (31), who headed up the kitchen on the day. A string quartet serenaded the guests while they ate. The Orangery was beautifully decorated with coral peonies and white roses, and guests were delighted with their personalised frosted shot glasses, which were later used to toast the happy couple.

Later that evening, the couple's families and friends enjoyed an evening of entertainment that included a caricaturist booth, a candy bar, fire performers mingling with the guests, a glitter bar for everyone to sparkle up their outfits, a casino, and a set by the well-known DJ M2theN. Undoubtedly the highlight of the evening was the surprise appearance of grammy award-winning country star Florence Dye-Walsh, who performed a set with her band. Ms Dye, who is married to country music legend Royce Walsh and lives in Nashville, is Charles Astley's niece.

A spectacular firework display in the grounds of Francis Court ended the unforgettable wedding celebrations, and each guest left with a mini hamper, including an exclusive olive oil blended in Italy by Mr Lattimore's cousin especially for the event and a hangover kit. Mr Lattimore and Mr Juke are honeymooning in Italy where they will host a reception for Mr Lattimore's family who were unable to make the journey for the wedding.

TV's Ryan Hawley will be back at Francis Court next

month when filming starts for Bake Off Wars. *Ryan has replaced Mike Jacob as a judge on the show and will join fellow judge Vera Bolt along with new presenters Hamilton Moore and Summer York for the eighth season of the popular baking show.*

———

I hope you enjoyed *A Cocktail to Die For*. If you did then please consider writing a review on Amazon or Goodreads, or even both. It helps me a lot if you let people know that you recommend it.

Will Bea and Perry get caught up in the middle of a Bake Off war? Find out in the next book in the *A Right Royal Cozy Investigation* series *Dying to Bake*. Pre-order it on Amazon now.

Want to know how Perry and Simon solved their first crime together? Then join my readers' club and receive a FREE short story *Tick, Tock, Mystery Clock* at https://www.-subscribepage.com/helengoldenauthor_nls or you can buy the ebook or paperback from Amazon.

For other books in the series take a look at the back of this book.

. . .

If you want to find out more about what I'm up to you can find me on Facebook at helengoldenauthor , Instagram at helengolden_author and TikTok at @helengoldenauthor.

Be the first to know when my next book is available. Follow Helen Golden on Amazon, Bookbub, and Goodreads to get alerts whenever I have a new release, preorder, or a discount on any of my books.

A BIG THANK YOU TO...

...my friends and family who continue to offer encouragement and support.

To my editor Marina Grout. As always you make my stories and characters better than I could do on my own.

To Ann, Ray, and my lovely friend Carolyn for being my additional set of eyes before I publish.

To my ARC Team. For the reviews. For the great feedback. For spotting mistakes. For being part of my support team. I appreciate everything you do for me.

To you, my readers. Your emails, social media comments, and reviews encourage me to keep writing. I appreciate your support more than you can imagine. I must mention two readers in particular, Pamela Court from Coon Rapids in Minnesota, USA, and Astrid Lowe who also lives in Minnesota, USA, who both won a competition to name a character each in this book. Thank you for taking part, and I hope you enjoy seeing your name in print.

As always, I may have taken a little dramatic license when it comes to police procedures, so any mistakes or misinterpretations, unintentional or otherwise, are my own.

CHARACTERS IN ORDER OF APPEARANCE

Perry Juke — Lady Beatrice's business partner and BFF.

Lady Beatrice — The Countess of Rossex. Seventeenth in line to the British throne. Daughter of Charles Astley, the Duke of Arnwall and Her Royal Highness Princess Helen. Niece of the current king.

Henry Greenhill — manager of Chasingham House Hotel and Spa.

Emma McKeer-Adler — Detective Chief Inspector, investigations team PaIRS.

Ellie Gunn — Francis Court's catering manager.

Claire Beck — Francis Court's human resources manager

Camile 'Cammy' Redmaine — Supermodel. The birthday girl. Suggested by reader Astrid Lowe.

Felicity 'Flick" Spencer — Friend of Bea's cousin, Caroline. One of 'the birthday girls'.

Barney Spencer — Flick Spencer's husband.

Mel Parks — Supermodel. One of 'the birthday girls'.

Vikki Carrington — Literary Agent. One of 'the birthday girls'.

Mercy Bright — American. One of 'the birthday girls'. Suggested by reader Pamela Court.

Lady Caroline Clifford — Lady Beatrice's cousin.

Andrew Parks — Mel Parks' father. Owner of Chasingham House

King James and Queen Olivia — King of England and his wife.

Simon Lattimore — Perry Juke's soon-to-be husband. Bestselling crime writer. Ex-Fenshire CID. Winner of cooking competition *Celebrity Elitechef*

Charles Astley — Duke of Arnwall. Lady Beatrice's father.

HRH Princess Helen — Duchess of Arnwall. Mother of Lady Beatrice. Sister of the current king.

François — server in The Stables restaurant at Chasingham House.

Isobel 'Izzy" McKeer-Adler — Emma's wife.

Richard Fitzwilliam — Detective Chief Inspector at *PaIRS (Protection and Investigation (Royal) Service)* an organisation that provides protection and security to the royal family and who investigate any threats against them. *PaIRS* is a division of *City Police*, a police organisation based in the capital, London.

Characters In Order Of Appearance

James Wiltshire — The Earl of Rossex. Lady Beatrice's late husband killed in a car accident fifteen years ago.

Sam Wiltshire — son of Lady Beatrice and the late James Wiltshire, the Earl of Rossex. Future Earl of Durrland.

Roisin McNally — Simon Lattimore's best friend who works in Forensics at Fenshire Police.

Jarvis Freeth — barman at Space, the cocktail bar at Chasingham House.

Victor 'Vic' Meed — Detective Sergeant, Chase Police CID

Doctor Romaine — pathologist, Cotswolds regional police.

Nigel Blake — Superintendent at *PaIRS*. Fitzwilliam's and Adler's boss.

Alan Rivers — Detective Chief Inspector, Chase CID.

Ross Coles — Mercy's late husband.

Mrs Everett — Housekeeper, Chasingham House.

Lady Sarah Rosdale — Lady Beatrice's elder sister. Twin of Fred Astley. Manages events at Francis Court.

Daisy — Lady Beatrice's adorable West Highland Terrier.

Frederick (Fred) Astley — Earl of Tilling. Lady Beatrice's elder brother and twin of Lady Sarah Rosdale. Ex-Intelligence Army Officer. Future Duke of Arnwall.

ALSO BY HELEN GOLDEN

A short prequel in the series A Right Royal Cozy Investigation. Can Perry Juke and Simon Lattimore work together to solve the mystery of the missing clock before the thief disappears? FREE novelette when you sign up to my readers' club. See end of final chapter for details. Ebook only.

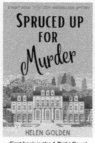

First book in the A Right Royal Cozy Investigation series. Amateur sleuth, Lady Beatrice, must pit her wits against Detective Chief Inspector Richard Fitzwilliam to prove her sister innocent of murder. With the help of her clever dog, her flamboyant co-interior designer and his ex-police partner, can she find the killer before him, or will she make a fool of herself?

Second book in the A Right Royal Cozy Investigation series. Amateur sleuth, Lady Beatrice, must once again go up against DCI Fitzwilliam to find a killer. With the help of Daisy, her clever companion, and her two best friends, Perry and Simon, can she catch the culprit before her childhood friend's wedding is ruined?

The third book in the A Right Royal Cozy Investigation series. When DCI Richard Fitzwilliam gets it into his head that Lady Beatrice's new beau Seb is guilty of murder, can the amateur sleuth, along with the help of Daisy, her clever westie, and her best friends Perry and Simon, find the real killer before Fitzwilliam goes ahead and arrests Seb?

A Prequel in the A Right Royal Cozy Investigation series. When Lady Beatrice's husband James Wiltshire dies in a car crash along with the wife of a member of staff, there are questions to be answered. Why haven't the occupants of two cars seen in the accident area come forward? And what is the secret James had been keeping from her?

ALL EBOOKS AVAILABLE IN THE AMAZON STORE.

PAPERBACKS AVAILABLE FROM WHEREVER YOU BUY YOUR BOOKS.

ALSO BY HELEN GOLDEN

The fourth book in the A Right Royal Cozy Investigation series. Snow descends on Drew Castle in Scotland cutting the castle off and forcing Lady Beatrice along with Daisy her clever dog, and her best friends Perry and Simon to cooperate with boorish DCI Fitzwilliam to catch a killer before they strike again.

When the dead body of the event's planner is found at the staff ball that Lady Beatrice is hosting at Francis Court, the amateur sleuth, with help from her clever dog Daisy and best friend Perry, must catch the killer before the partygoers find out and New Year's Eve is ruined. Ebook only. Available in Vol 1 of Riddles, Resolutions and Revenge Anthology.

A murder at Gollingham Palace sparks a hunt to find the killer. For once, Lady Beatrice is happy to let DCI Richard Fitzwilliam get on with it. But when information comes to light that indicates it could be linked to her husband's car accident fifteen years ago, she is compelled to get involved. Will she finally find out the truth behind James's tragic death?

ALL EBOOKS AVAILABLE IN THE AMAZON STORE.

An unforgettable bachelor weekend for Perry filled with luxury, laughter, and an unexpected death. Can Bea, Perry, and his hen's catch the killer before the weekend is over?

Bake Off Wars is being filmed on site at Francis Court and everyone is buzzing. But when much-loved pastry chef and judge, Vera Bolt, is found dead on set, can Bea, with the help of her best friend Perry, his husband Simon, and her cute little terrier, Daisy, expose the killer before the show is over?

PAPERBACKS AVAILABLE FROM WHEREVER YOU BUY YOUR BOOKS.

Printed in the USA
CPSIA information can be obtained
at www.ICGtesting.com
LVHW090203160224
772029LV00012B/124